GR

Matt is the youngest ~~~~~~~~~~~~~~~~~~~~~~~~~~ nagged and shouted at ~~~~~~ ~~~ ~~ not very bright and a little clumsy. But he has his own secret place, a disused barn, and it's to there he decides to run away and hide.

In the gloomy evening light he gets a terrible fright when he discovers that someone else has also discovered his hideout. The frail old lady is confused and exhausted but refuses to leave the barn. Nicknaming her Granny Apple because of her wrinkled cheeks, Matt fetches her food and blankets to keep her warm.

Despite the developing relationship between the two runaways, Matt's efforts to look after the old lady and keep her whereabouts secret lead to near disaster. In an exciting climax Matt discovers that he is not the outcast he thought he was.

Margaret Tufton was born in Norfolk and moved to Worcestershire, where she still lives, when she married. She is an English teacher by training and continues to teach part-time. She has four children and is a member of a local poetry group. *Granny Apple* is her first novel.

Granny Apple

MARGARET TUFTON

ILLUSTRATED BY NEIL REED

PUFFIN BOOKS

PUFFIN BOOKS

Published by the Penguin Group
Penguin Books Ltd, 27 Wrights Lane, London w8 5tz, England
Viking Penguin, a division of Penguin Books USA Inc.
375 Hudson Street, New York, New York 10014, USA
Penguin Books Australia Ltd, Ringwood, Victoria, Australia
Penguin Books Canada Ltd, 2801 John Street, Markham, Ontario, Canada l3r 1b4
Penguin Books (NZ) Ltd, 182–190 Wairau Road, Auckland 10, New Zealand

Penguin Books Ltd, Registered Offices: Harmondsworth, Middlesex, England

First published by Viking Kestrel 1989
Published in Puffin Books 1991
1 3 5 7 9 10 8 6 4 2

Printed in England by Clays Ltd, St Ives plc
Filmset in Baskerville (Linotron 202)

CHAPTER ONE

It was Friday evening again and already they were nagging him. Matt found the news very boring; grey old men walking about with briefcases, faces yacking about a common market (he had visions of bony cows tied up on open land, swishing at the flies with their filthy tails, of clapped-out lorries and piles of apples): '...*the Prime Minister pressed strongly for a budget refund*...'; the Navy were going to order another nuclear-powered, hunter-killer submarine (he didn't think he'd like to go on a sub, not under water; you'd be trapped, run out of air, die...). He shuddered, thinking about it.

'Can't you ever sit still? All right, Bridgie, get a cloth and mop it up. Matthew, just sit still; you've done enough damage. And sit up; your elbows should be by your sides, they're not wings...' and so on. Nag, nag, nag.

His sister shouldn't have put her beaker so close; he always got the blame.

Gosh, look at that: '...*late last night. Neighbours raised the alarm and broke in to drag the children clear of the flames.*

Forty-two-year-old Martin Jarvis later said . . .'

'Can't you even say sorry? How would you like water all over your dinner?' His mother was still nagging.

'Sorry,' mumbled Matt, eyes riveted on the television, watching a clergyman arriving at court – to contest the doorstep delivery of wine. Wonder what it's like to get drunk, thought Matt. Some of his classmates said they'd been drunk. The nearest he'd ever got to it was a glass of cider at Sunday lunch. Rob's dad got drunk most nights, Rob said, but he'd gone inside again last week. Stealing. Rob didn't seem bothered. Wouldn't it be great if his mum and dad went to prison! He could do what he liked then, especially if his brother and sister weren't there either. Would he miss them at all?

Hal, at seventeen, seemed to have little time to spare these days; when he wasn't working up in his room he was OK. But everything was easy for him; he didn't care two hoots what people thought. He might be a lawyer; he wasn't sure yet. Something brainy, anyway. Bridget wasn't too bad, he supposed, but she was a girl. At fifteen she seemed to spend all her time mooning around or worrying about what she looked like or giggling with Mum. She didn't like school much – but at least she wasn't in the bottom stream. He was. You weren't supposed to know, but what did they think you were, dummy-heads?

'Matt? Stop dreaming.'

He peered defiantly from under his heavy fringe and tucked in to his pudding. The weather forecast was on: '. . . *turning much colder. This low in the Atlantic is moving across* . . .' The chart was a mass of close black circles. The man plonked clouds and raindrops here and there, turned and beamed. Dad switched off the telly.

'So much for my weekend's gardening. Right. Who's on washing-up? No takers? Matt . . .'

'No thanks, there's a programme . . .'

'There's always a programme, my love. How about helping for a change?' Mum again. As usual.

'Why can't Hal and Bridgie?'

'Because they've got homework and you haven't.'

'So?'

'So you could help.'

'It's always *me*.'

'OK. You go and fetch a book and do some reading for half an hour; Dad and I'll do it.'

'Reading, reading, reading, that's all you ever think about. I hate reading.'

'Matt . . .'

'I'm not *going* to . . .'

'Matt . . .'

'Oh, all right. But I'm stopping at five to seven; I'm not missing my programme.'

Matt crashed out and banged the door on the remains of the evening meal, the cottage kitchen, the muddle and the chatter. Bodger, the labrador, half got up to follow him, heard a scraping of plates and thought better of it. Pinocchio, the cat, curled his tail more firmly around him, and continued to doze by the Rayburn.

Up in his bedroom, Matt brooded. How much money had he got? He went to his cash-box and began to count it. £1.54. Surely he had more than that? He counted it again. This time he made it £1.74. And then £1.72. He gave up. It wasn't nearly enough, anyway. Rob said he wanted £2.50 for the record. And then there would be problems explaining it to Mum and Dad; they didn't like him buying things at school. He flicked on his tape recorder: '. . . *I know by your smile that you love me . . .*' Huh; not many smiles since he'd come home. Do this, do that, do . . .

'Matt? Turn that row off and start some reading, child.'

7

Yack, yack, yack. Child, indeed. He was thirteen, nearly. Where should he live when he left home? Wherever it was, he would take Bodger. Good bloke, Bodger. 'He doesn't care if I'm thick...' Sighing, Matt yanked out a paperback, opened it at random, smacked down his open hand across it to flatten the spine and began to read, leaving out the hard words. All the while, as he rocked on the back legs of his chair, his other hand idly twisted and pulled a loose thread from his shirt button. The button fell off.

'I'm going to take Bodger out.'

'Keep him on the lead if there are any sheep about and don't let him get into the stream. And make sure that you wear your boots and your old anorak; I don't want your school one all covered in mud.'

'Oh, Mum; my school one's warmer.'

'Tough. Have a nice time!'

'Bye.'

Dog in tow, Matt headed off across the fields, the telly programme forgotten. ('Thank goodness,' thought his mother as she watched the ecstatic dog racing about in the dusk. 'Bodger's good for Matt; life's tough at the bottom of the heap.' She sighed.) Boy and dog gallumphed on in the fading light. The wind was cold.

'Fetch; fetch boy!'

Bodger raced after the stick, ears flapping beside his head, golden tail revolving ecstatically. Jamming his anchors on, he grabbed the stick, rushed back to Matt and dropped it at his feet. 'Good boy, Bodge; good boy. Fetch...' The stick arced out again. The dog raced away. The game went on until both wearied of it.

'OK, Bodge; let's go across to Gallows End. Come on, I'll race you.'

They took off, boy and dog, across fields, along tracks, over streams, on and on, sometimes fast as crazy, sometimes idling and kicking, throwing stones in the stream. Bodger leapt in and out, wet and dripping, happy.

Eventually they arrived at their most secret place, the old cottage. Lying in a hollow in the middle of rather neglected fields, served only by an overgrown and disused track blocked by sagging, heavy gates, the place was quite deserted. The little cottage was derelict, roofed only by rotting timbers to which a few forlorn tiles clung; the chimney-stack had begun to crumble and an elder tree grew from its shoulders; the floorboards had rotted or been eaten away, the windows were broken and tacked about with rags. It was totally unsafe. But beside it, the small barn offered more scope. Disused for years, it yet had a wide brick hearth, a roof that was more or less weatherproof, a dry stone floor and light from high openings as well as from the enormous doorway. The rafters were way up, shadowy, and sparrows gossiped and fought there. In the bales of rotting straw were rustles and squeaks. Defunct household articles had been slung there — two or three old chairs riddled with woodworm, a table with a broken leg, an old copper, rusting tools, packing-cases, farm junk of all sorts.

Bodger and Matt soon got down to ratting.

'Where is it? Fetch it out, Bodge. Fetch it out . . .'

Bodger whined with excitement, dug into the straw, scraped and tore at the old bales. The dust flew, the air was thick with it. Bodger sneezed and shook his heavy head. Matt jumped about, slipped and slid on the straw, poked and prodded with an old iron bar. At last, exhausted, they both collapsed on the floor, Bodger licking Matt's face in an excess of love.

'Shove off, Bodge. Let me up.'

Matt struggled up and started throwing bits of stick and rubbish at an old tin can in the fire recess. The sticks began to form a little heap. It was then that Matt saw that he had split his anorak, his school anorak, from shoulder to hem. Only too well could he imagine the row there would be at home – again.

'Bodge?' For an instant he threw his arms around the dog's panting body and buried his face in the dusty fur. Straightening up, he drew his dirty sleeve across his eyes and sat still for a moment. And then the idea burst into his mind like an exploding firework. He would make himself a hideout, a sort of refuge. Here was this place, secret; nobody else ever came. He was fed up with being got at, nagged at, shouted at. It wasn't his fault he was stupid. He chucked another stick at the can. Quite a heap of sticks. It was difficult to see now, almost dark. If he had a match . . . Yes, if he had a match he could make a fire. And cook maybe? He wasn't too good at cooking and Mum might notice if he took too much. It needed planning, but yes, if they went on at him, on and on, made him do everything, he'd run away. Yes; he would. If they couldn't be bothered to love him they could get lost. Or rather he would.

He would run away!

CHAPTER TWO

'Where are you going with those matches?'

'I'm just borrowing them; I want to do an experiment.'

'Well, you can just put them back. Your last experiment nearly burnt the house down, my love!'

Matt sighed. It was proving very difficult to gather things together to take to his hideout; with the rain pouring down all morning, there seemed to be people all over the cottage, noticing. Nor did he really know what to take.

'Bodge? Wake up, Bodge. Here; come here!' He rugger-tackled the dog and rolled with him under the kitchen table, scattering stools left and right. Bodger clamped his jaws round a good big mouthful of jersey and hung on; Matt patted his feet to make him dance about but he wouldn't let go. Growling playfully, the dog dug in with his back legs, braced himself and slithered backwards on the tiles.

'Bodge! Drop it; drop. You're making a hole . . .'

'Matt . . .'

'OK; I'm going.'

Matt clattered out of the kitchen and up to his bedroom. Carefully closing the door, he pulled the bed away from the wall. Behind were several polythene bags, two of them bulging. One ear cocked for sounds of people coming, he inspected his spoils.

'Knife, string, newspaper, baked beans . . . I'll need a tin-opener; I'll pinch the one in the Dormobile . . . bacon, eggs, tin of milk, saucepan . . .' Quietly Matt muttered over the things he had, untroubled by the things he hadn't, such as something to wash up with. Bread was a problem, though. He would have to remember to take some each time he went. And how long did bacon keep?

Footsteps!

Quick as a flash, Matt shoved everything back, scraped his bed across the carpet and threw himself on to the floor with his Airfix plane. Hal barged in.

'It says "Knock" on the door.'

'Sorry. Have you pinched my stapler?'

'Why me?'

'You were doing a project, weren't you?'

'Yes, but I haven't got it.'

'What are you doing up here?'

'Nothing much.'

'You've got those transfers on crooked.'

'So?'

'Just thought you'd like to know.'

Hal pushed off, yelling for Bridgie to hand over his stapler.

Where was he? Yes, tin-opener.

Matt clattered down the stairs and leapt out into the rain to the shed, got as far as the back door, and remembered he would need the van keys. Back he came, dripping water all over the kitchen, grabbed the keys from the back of the door and charged off again. He banged the door behind him but it didn't shut. In the shed once more, he came across another snag. Dad.

'Just the chap I want. Hold this steady a mo' while I screw this plate on.'

Dad was making something for the Scouts. Matt was a Scout, of sorts.

'Can I go now?'

'No, hang on. There's the other side.'

'Oh, Dad; I was doing something.'

Matt hopped from one foot to the other in his impatience and knocked over the jar of screws with his elbow.

'Sorry.'

'You will be.' Dad grinned.

Matt picked up the scattered screws.

'Now can I go?'

'What's your hurry? Nearly done. Keep it steady. Thanks; that's got it.' Dad straightened up and looked thoughtful. 'Did you want something?'

'Yes. Well, sort of...' Matt eyed him doubtfully and curled a wood shaving round his finger. 'I want something from the van. I think I left it there...'

'Feel free. It's not locked.'

Matt nipped into the Dormobile, found the tin-opener and slipped it into his pocket. So far, so good. He whizzed back to the cottage through the rain. Now, what else?

Lunch was over. Matt zipped himself into his anorak, whistled up Bodger, and slipped out of the side gate with his two bulging polythene bags. Everyone except Mum was watching the rugger match on telly; Bridget was bananas on sport. Mum was ironing.

Gosh, it was cold. He wished he'd brought his gloves but if he went back he'd be bound to be nobbled. Anyway, he hadn't a clue where they were.

13

'Hey, Bodge! Heel. Don't you go chasing off.'

Bodger amiably came loping back, soaking wet from the long grass, and shook himself.

'Hey, you biff; that's me you're drowning.'

Bodger grinned, hanging out his pink tongue.

The cottage was on the edge of the village and their way led through fields and paths, an occasional copse. As Matt went, he planned what he would do. There was a tea-chest in the barn. If he put it on its side up in the recess of that deep window, could rats climb up to it? No, surely they couldn't. That's what he'd do. Put it up there and stack all the food and stuff in. Maybe there'd be something he could fix in front of it, a piece of wood or chicken wire or something. Well, it didn't matter, most of his stuff was in tins; safe enough. He wouldn't have time to make a fire this time – anyway, he hadn't got matches. What else would he need? Water. Where was there any water ... He did cross a stream on the way; no, that wouldn't do. It might have a dead sheep in it for all he knew. Water. That was a problem. He couldn't carry it all from home, could he? It'd be jolly heavy. Pump! There was a pump behind the old cottage.

'I wonder if it still works!'

Matt was talking to himself in his excitement. He knew that sometimes you had to pour water down the collar of the shaft and keep pumping. He had seen them priming old Mrs Wilkins' pumping in the village last summer. Oh well, he'd just have to see.

'Bodge, I'm cold. My hands are just about frozen to these bags. It's all right for you; you've got a fur coat.'

He was nearly there. He could see the chimney of the cottage, the gable end of the barn, the old door.

Suddenly Matt frowned. Surely he'd tied that door to the hasp? Surely.

'I know I did,' Matt muttered. He stopped and considered. 'I *did*.'

He had never known anyone come here but himself. There had never been the slightest sign of anyone else in all the time he and Bodger had been coming here. You couldn't see the place from any road – it lay in the hollow. Perhaps a farmer came past occasionally, but why would a farmer go into the barn? It wasn't really good enough to store things in; anyway, it was miles from the farm and full of junk. Perhaps someone had just sheltered there. Oh well, probably some walker, waiting for the rain to blow over, or ... Then he looked at Bodger. The dog stood, his nose reaching towards the dark inside of the barn; his mane and the hair along his back were standing up on end. He gave a low growl, looked at Matt, and then put his head down a little, tensed, and softly growled again.

Matt shivered, and not with cold this time. What should he do?

He put the two bags down very gently behind a rusted water tank; they crackled alarmingly in the stillness. Moving as quietly as he could, he tiptoed slowly underneath the window, the sill a little above his head. He daren't risk jumping up; it would be too noisy. He looked around and risked a single snap of his fingers. Bodger reluctantly left the doorway and came to his side; he gave a soft whimper.

'Quiet,' whispered Matt into the dog's ear.

He saw a baulk of timber, an old fence post, and gently leaned it against the brick wall, beneath the window. He reached up with his fingers and hooked them over the window ledge, put his right foot on top of the post, pressed on it carefully, found it firm and used it as a step up. Straightening his leg slowly, he raised himself until he could peer through the dirty, greened glass, or what was left of it. He could see very little. A shaft of dim light lay across the dirty floor from the open doorway, but everything else was in shadow.

He listened. Bodger moved restlessly in the rubbish below. Could he hear anything? Nothing. Then . . . yes! No; it was a branch flapping against the wall. He pressed his face closer to the glass, shut out the light behind him by cupping his hands against the sides of his face. He peered through the gloom. There was something pale over in the corner. Pale? He tried to remember what was usually in that corner. Straw was pale, but . . . no, the heap of straw was bigger than that. What else was . . . but there was no time for more. The pale thing was coming towards him. Matt flinched and the post slipped sideways. Even as he leapt clear, Matt felt his stomach knot with fear.

There was someone there.

CHAPTER THREE

He landed in a tangle of weeds. Good job it was March and the stingers were dead, thought Matt, and then froze ... There was a hesitant, shuffling, dragging noise. It was inside the barn, coming towards him. Bodger gave one deep, threatening bark; and then yelped as Matt hit him across the nose.

'Quiet,' he hissed. 'Shurrup, Bodge...'

Bodger strained and whimpered, his ears crinkled up, his nose thrust forward. He looked at Matt for permission to go.

Matt fixed his eyes on the entrance to the barn. What should he do? Run? Or stay ... Don't be silly, he told himself, it's only someone sheltering from the rain. But it wasn't raining any more. Well, the cold then; or they've come to fetch something.

He tried to remember what was in the barn. Was there anything worth fetching? A few mouldy bales of straw, bits of rusty machinery, rotten sacks, old boxes, bits of timber, broken doors, an iron mangle, maybe a broken . . .

'Bodge! *No*, Bodge! Heel . . .!'

It was too late. Unable to contain himself any longer, Bodger had rushed into the barn, yelping in excitement now, his tail whizzing round in circles. He disappeared through the doorway and there was a muffled thump and a thin cry. And silence.

Matt ran. What had they done to Bodge? He'd kill them. If they'd touched Bodge . . .

Coming into the barn from the light outside, at first he could see nothing. He stood still and listened, straining his ears for any sound. There was an anxious whine: Bodger. And then there he was, thrusting a wet nose into Matt's hand and whimpering. 'Come on,' he seemed to be saying. 'Come on . . .' But Matt couldn't come on – his knees seemed to have turned to jelly and his neck felt damp. He shivered. Something moved in front of him. As his eyes grew used to the gloom, he could see a hunched shape – a sheep? No, it was human. It was trying to get up. It had some sort of long gown on and a pale cloud round its head; and the clouded head was swinging and jerking, swinging and jerking, like a pendulum.

'I don't believe in ghosts; I don't believe in ghosts . . .' Matt's eyes were round with fear and his heart seemed to be banging about in his ribs as if it were trying to break out. 'I don't believe . . .' Then he noticed Bodger's tail, wagging gently and reassuringly. The dog looked up at him; then he moved forward to bend his heavy head and give an encouraging lick to . . . whatever it was. Matt let out a huge gasp of air in his relief. It was, or rather she was, a lady; a very old lady with a mass of wispy white hair. Just an old lady, but 'Why are you crawling about the floor?' Matt rushed to help her up. 'Are you all right? Have you hurt yourself?'

She didn't seem to see him. Perhaps she's deaf,

thought Matt. He shouted loudly, in her ear.

'Are you all right?'

'Hmm?' She turned her constantly moving head to look at him; or through him. Matt wasn't sure.

Matt was tall for his age, and strong. He gripped her firmly under the armpits and prepared to heave her to her feet – and nearly fell over backwards. She weighed nothing, nothing at all; and she was soft – like a kitten, thought Matt, surprised. Kittens were soft, floppy and furry. The cloth under his hands was soft, fluffy . . .

'Thank you, love; that's kind you are . . .' A thin little voice.

She stood there, swaying a little, held by his two hands.

'. . . so kind.'

What was he to do with her? She'd fall over again in a minute.

'Bodge, stop it! You'll have her over.'

Bodger was pushing against her, thrusting his nose up under her hand and then sneezing and shaking his head.

'I bet you already have, haven't you.' Matt was stern. That's what had happened; Bodge must have rushed in and jumped up to greet her – and knocked her flying. What should he do with her? And what on earth was she wearing? It was dirty and torn with sticky-looking holes, dark-edged, worse around the hem. It dragged about her, woolly dingy . . . pink? Why, it was a dressing-gown. A dressing-gown? What on earth . . .

'. . . so tired, love. Could I . . . sit down?'

'OK.' Matt looked around. Where? Where could she sit? 'Come on, over here; I'll help you.' He kept his right arm round her, under her arm, and with his left hand held her other arm just below the elbow. Gingerly at first. But then, as she wavered and stumbled, he held her closely, firmly, and steered her across to a bale of old straw that had fallen from a stack.

'OK?'

'Hmm?' She didn't seem to understand; constantly weaving and bobbing her head she leaned forward, her hand behind her ear. 'Hmm?'

'Are you OK?'

No answer.

Matt shouted again, 'Are you all right?'

The pale eyes focused on him.

'You don't need to shout. You young people can't seem to live without noise, can't seem to live...' Her eyes wandered away again and she muttered something too low for Matt to catch.

She was shivering. Well, Gordon Bennett, it was too bloomin' cold to be wandering about in a dressing-gown, especially one with holes in it. And look at her feet; she had slippers on her feet. Slippers? Well, sort of – remains, more like. They were caked in mud, all the fur round the top had gone soggy and yukky; some of it looked like cow dung.

What on earth was she doing here? Perhaps she had run away, too. Matt grinned.

'Have you run away?'

'Run away?'

'Yes. Have you run away?'

She looked puzzled; and then the light went out of her eyes and she looked ... inward? Matt couldn't explain it to himself; she just wasn't there any more, she was somewhere else, somewhere ... frightening. The old lady shivered. 'It was frightening; I couldn't ... I couldn't ... and now I can't find it, and ... I don't remember...' She fell silent, shaken by bouts of violent shivering that rocked her thin body. The silence stretched between them like a black hole. Then, 'They tried to stop me going, they tried to stop me...'

'But you went.' Matt felt a new respect for her. 'You ran away.'

Bodger came up, snorting the dust out of his nose, shook himself and settled at the old lady's feet. After a while he relaxed and rolled on to his side, resting his head on the slippers.

Well, at least that would keep her feet warm, for starters. What ought he to do? Keep her warm. That much was obvious. But how?

They had just had a talk at Scouts on survival. Matt hadn't listened much. He had been too busy tickling Jeremy's neck with a feather. Jeremy had a red neck; come to that, he was pretty red all over. He had ginger hair and freckles, and a posh voice, and posh manners. Other kids would have turned round and socked him one, but not Jeremy – that was half the fun, trying to make him, but ... Oh, shut up, said Matt to himself. Concentrate. Keeping warm ... Use anything, the man said, anything; you had to con ... cons ... con-something your body heat in emergencies, because of shock. Was this an emergency? Was the old lady shocked? She didn't look shocked. When Mum was shocked, or Bridget, their faces went all stern and tight, disapproving. And often it seemed to be his fault, and he felt guilty. Well, he wasn't feeling guilty today, and the old lady didn't look at all disapproving; she didn't look anything much, in fact she looked sort of blank. Perhaps there could be an emergency without shock; and she had said she was cold.

OK. Anything, the man said. Matt looked around. Old straw, yes; and sacks? 'Jolly dusty, but thick,' he murmured. An old rick-cover; no, that was no good, canvas doesn't bend properly, but ...

Matt made a start. He lugged some bales around until he had built a sort of big armchair. Then he dragged over the remains of the rick-cover, knocking out some of the dirt and old plaster on the way, and draped it over the erection from the back to the floor. Great; that would stop it being so scratchy. Actually the 'chair' was so wide you could sleep in it, thought Matt. Oh well, maybe that was a good idea. Right; now what?

'Bodger, what *are* you doing?'

Bodger had taken an enormous interest in the proceedings, and now that they appeared to be completed he leapt up on to the seat, turned round a few times, and finally flopped down with a satisfied 'woomph' and prepared to sleep.

'No, Bodge, get off. It's not for you; it's for . . .' Who? I wonder what she's called, thought Matt. He glanced over to the old lady and saw her struggling to get up.

'Cold, so cold . . .'

He went over to help her.

'Good dog; nice old fellow, warm.'

Well, yes, he was. Matt steered her across to the . . . what had they called it in that stately home? Day-something . . . day-bed.

The old lady sat carefully beside Bodger, and then leaned against the side; she smiled a little and put her hand on the dog's head. Bodger shoved up, never one to miss a bit of attention. He sighed with pleasure and flopped his head into her lap, moved to a more comfortable position. This was bliss. He flapped his tail a couple of times, lazily.

Matt lugged up more straw bales to pack around the day-bed; he didn't want the old lady to fall through them, though she seemed nearly asleep.

Sacks next.

There were a couple over the old mangle, another on a rusty nail. Three, of sorts. Not very many. He took them out to the door and gave them a good bashing against the wall and shook them thoroughly. Bits of straw, clouds of dust, flew up – blew back into the barn.

'Biff; should have looked to see which way the wind was blowing.'

Matt took them in and put the biggest one round the

old lady's shoulders; it looked as if it might easily slip off. The other two he laid over her knees. Gosh, it was cold; and it was growing darker. If only he'd brought matches, he could have made a fire. That would warm the place up; and be a bit more cheerful . . .

Matt shivered. The corners of the barn were all in shadow now; the only light slanted down from two high windows at the end and in through the doorway. A rising wind made a little whirling straw-dance in the entrance.

Next time he would bring matches. He began gathering bits of straw and stick, setting them in a wigwam shape in the broken grate. He glanced across at the old lady. She seemed to be murmuring to Bodger. Matt went outside and fetched in some broken wood fencing, two or three short branches, the remains of a handle from some tool. As he dropped them down by the fireplace, the old lady started up violently.

'No!' She seemed terrified. 'No! No, no, no . . .' Her voice died away and she started to shake uncontrollably. 'No,' she whispered, and two or three difficult tears tracked slowly down her pale face.

'No?' Matt went to her. 'No what? What is it?'

She clung to him.

'Don't,' she begged him, 'don't.'

'Don't what?' Matt was mystified. 'I'm not doing anything. But,' as he looked at the sky outside, 'I'll have to go soon.' Go soon; the words echoed slowly through his mind. Go soon. The old lady – where would she go? He'd never thought. 'Where are you going?' and, more loudly, 'Do you want me to come with you?'

Bodger heard the anxiety in his voice and scrambled down to stand against him, pushing a little.

'Where . . .'

But the old lady gripped his arm, oddly strong, fierce.

'Here. I'm staying here . . .' Then it was as if a cloud

23

passed over her eyes, and 'The bear, the bear . . .'; her voice trailed away.

'But you *can't* stay, not here.'

Matt didn't know what to do.

'I'm staying; I'm going in.'

'But how long for? How long are you staying here?' What did she mean, 'going in'?

She smiled at him suddenly, as if she had known him all her life.

'I shall be quite all right. I shan't be gone long.' She looked away into the shadows. 'Now don't make a fuss, dear. There's no need to worry your mother; we won't tell anyone where I am. Least said, soonest mended. Promise? Promise, Charlie?'

Puzzled, Matt didn't actually say anything. He gave a slight nod.

She patted his cheek.

'That's my boy. Now, let me explain what I'm doing.'

CHAPTER FOUR

The old lady settled herself and lapsed into thought.
Bodger sat down abruptly, scratched his ear, shook
himself, and then rose and ambled off into the shadows,
barely visible in the gloom. His progress was punctuated
by rustles and occasional sneezes. Matt stood, unde-
cided; as he waited for the old lady to speak he was
aware of some unease nagging at the edges of his mind...

'You see, I...'

It was difficult to hear what she said. Her head was
down, moving gently from side to side, over and over; her
voice was thin, thread-like, drifting sometimes into
silence, though she seemed not to notice; the thumb of
one hand constantly fretted the other. Matt found
himself fascinated by those hands – nervous, the thin

25

skin folded and wrinkled, paper-dry. They didn't look strong. How would she manage?

Nothing she said made sense to him, just snatches of half-sentences, leading nowhere, fear and bewilderment in her eyes, over and over again something about a bear and not knowing, not meaning to be a nuisance . . . Then her voice strengthened, and she looked straight at Matt.

'Do you think we could have a cup of tea? I'd like that. A cup of tea . . . It's so cold . . .'

Tea? Where was he to get tea in the middle of nowhere? But the thought made Matt hungry. What wouldn't he give for a bar of chocolate. He searched his pockets, without much hope, for something to eat – and encountered the hard metal of the filched tin-opener. Tin-opener? Of course.

'Would you like something to eat?'

'Eat?'

She seemed puzzled.

'Mm; eat. I've got food outside. Bags of it. Hang on – I'll get it.'

He dashed out of the barn, to be struck by a chill, cutting wind. The sky was overcast and heavy, and the fading light had a strange underwater quality. Wasting no time, he grabbed his bags and went back inside.

He emptied provisions on to a tea-chest, selected a jar of lemon curd, prised off the lid, and spread some thickly on a slice of bread – using the handle of the tin-opener. Pity there was no margarine. Oh well, she probably wouldn't notice. He laid it on a piece of polythene bag that he tore off, and gave it to her – and then whipped his hands behind his back as he saw the colour of them.

'Oh thank you, love, that's kind . . .' and she took a slice, eating quietly and slowly; too slowly . . .

Shall I just leave her? Matt was worried. He must go home soon. It would be dark and his Mum would go off her rocker. Come on, come on, he urged her, silently.

26

What was he to do?

She had finished at last.

'Is there . . .' She looked a little shy, embarassed. 'Is there . . . any more?'

Matt spread two more slices, one for himself – after all, that's what he'd brought it for! – and another for her.

'Thank you.' She smiled.

Matt wolfed his piece down; and another. He looked at his watch. Not already! He would have to go.

'Are you ready to go now? Shall I come with you?'

'I'll be all right, love. Don't you worry about me. I'll manage fine now. Better; much better . . . If I could just have a cup of tea . . . so thirsty . . .'

There were two cans of coke. He gave her one. She looked bemused. Didn't she know how to open it? Her dry little hands turned it round and round. She'd fizz it up if she wasn't careful.

'Here. Give it to me.'

Matt took the can and carefully pulled off the ring, holding it well away from him. There was a froth of bubbles, boiling up.

'Quick! Drink it; drink some . . .'

He thrust it at the old lady who sipped the froth, wiped her lips with her other hand, and then tipped a little into her mouth.

'I must go.' Matt was desperate.

'Yes, dear, you go. I can manage quite well now.'

'But what about you?'

'Me?'

'What are you going to do?'

'Do?'

'Yes, do.' This was ridiculous.

'I'm not going to do anything, dear. I'm going to stay here and have a little sleep. Just have a little sleep . . . so tired . . . Tomorrow . . .'

'But you can't.'

'Why, dear?'

'It's not ... suitable.' Matt scrabbled for a word. 'It's not a ... home.'

For a moment she looked a little sad, lost. Then, 'I'll manage, dear. I'm a good manager – the war taught us that ...' War? What war? '... the times we had down at the centre when the Jerries went over; really cosy, it was.'

She began to arrange the sacks more to her liking, spreading one along the bales, stuffing some loose straw under one end for a thin pillow; and then she lay down.

Smiling, sleepy, she murmured, 'Just pull the others over me, dear ... That's right, that's ...' – her eyelids drooped a little – '... lovely. Night, Charlie dear. It's time you were in bed too, like your old Gran.' And as easily as a leaf falling to the ground, she was asleep.

Matt looked at her lying there, like a child. Trusting him. An odd, unfamiliar feeling stirred in Matt and he dashed an angry hand over his eyes.

He really must go.

'Bodge? Here ...'

Bodger surfaced through the darkness and the dust, and together they left for home – both quiet for once, absorbed in their own thoughts. After tea, Matt decided, he would go back with some blankets.

The cottage windows spilled shafts of light out on to the wind, flickering along the bare branches of the tossing willow and pointing the few whirling leaves with drops of flame. Matt's fingers, balled tightly in his anorak pockets, were numb with cold; his forehead ached and his legs were frozen. Framed by the windows, he could see Bridgie's fair head close to Hal's, huddled over a board-game; Dad was leaning forward from his crossword to put another log on the fire; and in the kitchen his mother glanced at the clock and then bent to the oven door. Great! Hot scones for tea! Matt tore along the path, collided with the dog who had taken a flying leap over the flower-bed, and crashed into the dustbin – his hands still wedged hopelessly in his pockets. The back door flew open; Bodger gave him a passing lick and dashed inside. Mum looked at him, the oven-glove dangling in her hand.

'Matt, what *are* you doing? Do you know what time it is? I don't like you wandering about in the dark like this. Come on, get up and come inside ...' And then, 'What have you done to your chin?'

Struggling to his feet, Matt was aware that it hurt; maybe he had hit it on the milk crate.

Once inside, 'Go and wash yourself and let's see to that cut.' His Mum was busy getting the scones.

Matt inspected the damage in the mirror over the basin. Not too bad. Ouch! Gosh, it was agony putting his numb hands in the hot water. Gingerly he moved them to and fro, then yanked off a wadge of cotton wool and dabbed at the blood.

'Here, let's see.' His mother took over, swabbing off the blood and dirt – 'How d'you *get* so dirty!' – and dabbing the wound with antiseptic.

'Ow, don't! It stings! Mum ...'

'Of course it stings. Keep *still*, Matt, we don't want it festering. Now, just clear up in here and sort yourself out and then we'll have tea. We've been waiting for you. Out of the way, Bodge; you stay in here till your feet dry.'

Matt was in bed. At last it seemed quiet. His mum and dad had gone to bed half an hour or so ago. There was no sound. No lights. Now. Now was the time. As quietly as he could he slid, fully dressed, from his bed and opened the window, pushing it back against the wind.

From his cupboard he took out three camp blankets he had hidden there earlier, and the old zipped sleeping-bag that nobody used now. One by one he dropped them out

29

into the dark. Lucky the wind had dried the path! The blankets whirled off sideways like huge grey bats, and draped themselves against the hedge; the sleeping-bag flumped on to a rose bush. There was a noise in the utility-room below him; Bodger put an exploring nose under the cat-flap. Matt froze. Minute after minute passed. Silence.

Carefully Matt climbed up on his desk, on to the window-sill; holding to the central bar, he put one wavering foot through and on to the guttering. He crouched, slithered the back foot through, slid it down the tiles, over the gutter, and felt about with it for the downpipe. Got it! Still hanging on like a limpet with his hands, he leaned forward, pressing his tummy to the sloping tiles and letting both legs hang over the edge until he could grip the pipe between his feet. Careful now. He moved one hand cautiously to grip the edge of the iron guttering, there – and put it splat into a mess of cold, slimy muck. He jerked back, instinctively; a loose tile clattered down over the gutter and shattered on the stone path.

Bodger exploded into life. Crashing his head through the cat-flap, he barked and barked, on and on. Enemies! Burglars! Fire! Help! I've got them, I've got them; I'll hold them till you come!

'Woof! Woof!' The night was splintered with jagged noise.

Shut up. Shut up. Please, Bodge . . .

Lights snapped on; footsteps. Matt clung to the drainpipe like a shadow, frozen with horror.

CHAPTER FIVE

Desperately, heart thudding, Matt hung on. Don't let them open my door; don't them come in!

There was a clatter as Bodger withdrew his head from the cat-flap; then he stuffed it out again and barked worse than ever. Don't, Bodge, don't!

The footsteps faded as someone went downstairs; a step creaked. More lights shone pale over the garden – from the dining-room, kitchen ... Another clatter as Bodger changed his tactics and rushed to seize the nearest human being. The utility-room light shone out for a moment; the barks had changed to excited whines. The back door was unlatched, opened ... Don't let the dog out; please don't let the dog out! He'll see me ... But Bodge was held by the scruff of his neck. Matt's father looked out into the dark and was satisfied. The trembling shadow that was Matt made no sound, a few short feet away above his father's head.

'There's no one there, Bodge. Now shut up and go to bed.'

Bodger gave a strangled whimper of protest and was pulled back inside. The lights went out one by one; footsteps padded up the stairs; muffled talking; then darkness. Silence once more.

Now what? Matt's arms ached with tension, his left leg was full of pins and needles. Dare he move? He would have to. As gently as he could, slowly, he eased himself over the gutter, slid inch by inch down the drainpipe, and finally put first one cautious foot and then the other on to the soft earth of the flower-bed. He stole out on to the path, turned to scribble out his footprints with his hand, and slid like a grey ghost over the grass to gather up the blankets and the sleeping-bag. There was no sound from the cottage.

Ten minutes later, Matt shifted his load from one arm to the other, nearly dropping his torch as he did so. Not that it was on; he was saving his batteries. He flexed his aching arm and then squawked as an unseen bramble clawed his face. He touched his cheek with his finger and licked it. Blood.

Matt sighed. Was he half-way yet? He didn't mind the dark. After all, he had slept out often enough in the summer; often. In the tent, under the apple trees. With Hal. And Hal was always asleep, so it was the same as being alone. Just the same; only ... And although the cottage was only across the garden in the dark, you couldn't see it, so it was the same as if it were miles away. It was the same as now, really, but ... Matt shivered. I like the dark, he told himself firmly, it's exciting.

What was that?

Matt's hair prickled on his scalp. He froze. A sound like a child's scream rose behind the hedge, desperate, and was suddenly cut off short. Matt found he was clutching the blankets to him, hiding his face. Slowly he peered above them, his eyes wide; he could see nothing, hear nothing. He didn't know what to do.

There was a rustle at the foot of the hedge. Matt didn't move. He couldn't. Something was being dragged. A fox darted across the track in front of him, dragging a rabbit, and disappeared into the night.

Matt's whole body was wobbly with relief. He stumbled along until he came to a fallen tree where he sat for a while, wrapping one of the blankets around him and eating half a bar of chocolate he had meant to save till later.

The night was very dark and cold, full of sounds. The faint hum of traffic, miles and miles away; little rustlings and patterings; the wind whining through the bare hedgerows, tapping the few dry leaves that still clung there; an occasional owl's cry or the distant bark of a dog fox. It was eerie, sitting there with everyone else asleep, unconscious; only Matt alive in a huge pool of darkness.

He must get on, but he wanted Bodger, warm and friendly. Taking life as it came, loving and comfortable. For a moment Matt considered going back – after all, what would it matter? The old lady would be asleep. She might not even be there. And then he would have to go into that barn all alone, dark and damp and secret. He only had a small torch. He could see it now, the shadows flickering and jumping at him, the beams, the dangling rope-ends . . . Gallows End. Why was it called Gallows End? Matt's heart began to thud . . .

Oh shut up, he told himself. Get on with it. You've done all right so far. (Just, said another corner of his mind.) Shut up. Shut up.

Matt stood up and sorted out his gear into a more manageable bundle, putting the blankets inside the sleeping-bag and slinging it over his shoulder like a sack. He strode off, perhaps rather faster than before.

The night wore on.

Crossing the stream, Matt lost his footing in the shifting shadows and went in up to his waist. The blankets were safe, which was lucky, but his wet jeans clung to him like a skin of ice. He stumbled on.

*

33

Despite his fears, it was almost a relief when he reached the barn. Too cold to hang about worrying, his only concern was to go inside, out of the thin, piercing wind.

He snapped on his torch and eased back the big wooden door. It was like going into an enormous black cave. He had often thought he would like to be an explorer. Now he wasn't so sure.

He had better call her. She would be frightened. What should he call her? He didn't know.

Cautiously he made his way in, shadows flickering and fanning around him.

'Are you there? It's me – Matt.'

No answer.

'Are you there?'

He tiptoed across to the straw bales. The soft circle of torchlight crept along the pale blocks of straw, reached the old rick-cover, picked out the oval fluff of a slipper lying on the floor; reached the tiny face. She was still there. Matt's tense body relaxed again. Still there. Was she all right? Was she . . . alive?

Matt bent over her. The little form lay still; she seemed like a child.

'Mrs . . . Granny? Are you all right?'

Still no answer.

Greatly daring, Matt pulled a sack a little away from her shoulder, touched her dry, powdery face.

'Granny?'

She stirred a little, sighed, snuggled her hand up under her cheek.

'Granny. 's me; Matt.'

Her eyes fluttered open. She smiled. Just lay there and smiled. Then she shrank down into the sacks and began to shake; her whole body rocked.

'Cold, Charlie; it's so cold.'

'I'm not Charlie. I'm Matt.' Why did she call him

Charlie? 'Matt.'

'Matt?'

Gently he helped her to sit up, brushed the wisps of straw off her, shook out the sacks and rick-cover, and set about making a more comfortable, warmer bed.

She sat on a straw bale watching him, still shivering, twisting her hands. Her hair looked a real mess, terrible, like a bird's nest; but he wasn't into hairdressing. Anyway, she didn't seem to mind – nice to find a lady who didn't fuss about her hair. Matt grinned at her with approval.

'There, that's better. Now you'll be warmer.'

Would she? She looked frozen. Maybe he should light his fire. He had brought matches this time; would she be able to look after it?

'Shall I light a fire?'

She looked at him. Some doubt stirred at the back of her eyes, a flicker of fear. She shook her head.

'No, love, no ... no flames ... the flames ...' She broke off and fumbled with a fold of her dressing-gown. 'I can't see. It's ...' She stood up, swaying a little; put up a hand in front of her eyes. 'It's ... all gone dark. I can't find ... It feels ...'

'Sit down.' Matt held her; a few difficult tears slipped down her cheeks. 'Sit down. You'll be all right. You're just cold. Here – sit down here.'

He managed to ease her down on to the bed. She sat there, staring in front of her. What could she see?

He gave her the other half of his bar of chocolate, unwrapping it from the shreds of silver paper. Fruit and nut; his favourite. The smell was magic! He couldn't bear it. He moved away and began arranging his fire in the broken grate, pausing occasionally to rub his fingers, stiff with cold. He couldn't feel his feet any more. He fumbled for the matches.

'No. No! Don't, love, don't! No ...'

35

She was stumbling towards him, tripping over her dressing-gown, reaching out.

'Please . . .'

Why? What was wrong with lighting a fire? He was jolly cold, too. It was all right for her; she hadn't got to go back out into that wind in soaked trousers and soggy wellies. Matt began to lose patience. He took out the box.

'No! No, no . . .'

She was almost shrieking now. Daft? Was she daft? What did she think would happen. It would be warm and cosy. Bright.

Bright? Yes, maybe she had a point. A light in the dark shines a very long way. Would it matter? Not to him; well, not much, though he would have to find another hideaway and he liked this one. But she had run away, too, and looking at her he doubted if she could run much further. Silly? Maybe; but brave. She had guts, his old lady. He grinned at her, put the matches back into his pocket.

'OK. You win.'

The urgency slipped from her.

'Good boy. Good . . . Come and sit down; come and sit with your old Gran.'

She settled herself again and patted the space beside her invitingly. Matt crossed over, sat down and unzipped the fat pouch of his anorak.

For a few minutes they sat together, friends, equals, not saying much and sipping the hot, sweet tea that Matt had brought in the picnic flask. The old lady folded both her hands around the warm plastic cup, smiling at this comfort. Matt drank in slow, small mouthfuls, feeling the heat curl down his long body . . .

It was time to go. Matt screwed up the flask, zipped it back safely in his pouch, and settled the old lady for sleep on the quilted sleeping-bag beneath the three fluffy blankets, drawing them carefully about her shoulders.

She closed her eyes and Matt crept out.

Hours later, it seemed, he slid frozen and weary through the shadowed village. Climbing the drainpipe seemed enormously difficult. Heaving himself through the narrow window, his anorak cord caught. Matt pulled and, as it suddenly gave, tumbled through with an almighty crash on to the floor.

That was it. Bodger broke into a positive ecstasy of barking; lights jumped on; doors opened; a perfect action replay.

Matt ripped off his anorak and kicked it under his desk, dived into bed and pulled his duvet up to his chin.

His door opened. Matt glued his eyes shut. Click. That was the light; he winced at the brightness against his closed lids. Matt lay still. He pretended he was dead. He soon would be.

There was a long and rather awful silence.

Then, 'Matt? Get up. Just where exactly have you been?'

'Been?' It came out as a squeak. 'Been?'

'Been. Your window's wide open, there's a howling gale; there's water on the floor; and you seem to have gone to bed in your wellies; wet wellies . . .'

Dad stood there and waited. He waited patiently until, finally, 'Out,' squeaked Matt. 'Just out.'

CHAPTER SIX

'What'd he say?'

It was no surprise to find that Matt had had another brush with authority; he was always in trouble for something or other, but this was classic. Hal was agog – he had to hear this!

After the disturbed night, they had all overslept. What with the scramble to feed the animals, feed themselves, be battered into some sort of cleanliness and respectability for church and find Bridgie's lost recorder (she had been nobbled to lead the tinies in their sung prayer, much to her annoyance!), there had been little time to hear the glorious details of Matt's midnight gaol-break. Now they were back. They gathered round the Rayburn, warming their hands with hot drinks.

'Go on. What happened?'

Matt didn't answer.

'Where did you go?' That was Bridgie. 'What did you go off in the dark for?'

Mum was upstairs, changing; Dad was outside, sawing logs. Matt considered ... He would have to say something.

'Dunno.'

'What d'you mean, "Dunno"? You *must* know. Where did you go? Why?' Bridgie was persistent.

'Why didn't you take us?' Hal was frankly envious. He would like to have gone out at night.

'Mind your own business. Leave me alone.' Matt looked a bit red in the face; he wasn't going to cry, was he?

No, he wasn't going to cry, but he felt he couldn't breathe. Questions, questions. Always questions. He wanted time to think. Why couldn't they leave him alone?

Bridgie looked at him, thoughtful.

'What did Dad do? Was he very angry?'

'Mm.' Matt didn't seem inclined to say any more about what his father had said; or done. Then, with sudden bravado, 'It's my window. Why shouldn't I go out if I want to? Nobody's ever told me not to.' Well, that was true, they hadn't. 'Anyway, what does it matter?'

Hal frowned a little; he was quite fond of his irritating kid brother.

'You could have been hurt, climbing down. That pipe's only held to the wall by a couple of rusty screws.'

'So?'

'So you were lucky.'

Very lucky – if only you knew how lucky! Matt shivered. He had managed not to tell his dad where he had been; just said he had been out for a walk to see what it was like and had fallen into the stream in the dark. Then his mum had taken over. Hot drink, hot-water bottle, clean sheets, warmed pyjamas, the works – but all rather silent, grim. His boots were drying now, wedged upside down in the rail of the Rayburn; they didn't half pong.

Hal looked at Matt over the rim of his mug. Funny kid. You never knew what he was thinking. He never said much about himself. Always in the wars, always in trouble; he never saw it coming. Everyone else would have been running for their lives – not Matt; he just hung around looking the other way until it flattened him. Brains of a peanut. He was still shivering.

'What's up? You cold?'

'No, not really.'

'You're shivering.'

'I'm not.'

'Just doing a jelly impression, are you?' But it was desperately cold outside. Was the kid OK? 'Perhaps you'll get pneumonia.'

'Why? What's numia?'

'Pneumonia, biff. A disease – like a bad cold and a high fever. You ache and shiver and burn; you can't breathe...'

'Shut up, Hal.' Bridgie was looking at Matt. 'He's just cold.'

'I'm not.'

'Well, it is jolly cold.'

'Hypothermia.'

'Huh?'

'Hypothermia; that's what old people get in this weather.'

'Hypo-what?' Matt put his mug down and rubbed at his front where he had spilt the hot cocoa. 'Hypo-what?'

'Hypothermia. People get it if they're lost on mountains in the snow.'

'But you said old people get it. What is it? Is it dangerous?'

'Mm. Can be. They get so cold they go into a sort of coma and die.'

'Die? Do old people die of it? Do they all get it?'

'Only if they can't keep warm. That's when they get it. If they can't afford coal or electricity, or if they have a fall and get stuck and can't get help.' Hal got up to go.

'*How* cold? How cold do they have to be before they get hypo . . . hypo . . . hy . . .'

'Hypothermia. I don't know – pretty cold but not all that; it's because they're old. Their bodies aren't so good at keeping warm.'

Matt shivered again.

Hal gave him a friendly shoulder charge.

'Think you're tough, do you? Oh, Mum! Mum!' He stood there, shaking exaggeratedly, rolling his eyes, chattering his teeth. 'Mum! Hypothermia's got me . . . Oh, Mum, I'm . . .'

'Shurrup.' Matt grabbed him. 'Shurrup!'

'Help! Mum, help! He's hugging me! He's gonna kiss me! He loves me . . . Gerroff, you turkey-brain. Gerroff . . . ow!'

They crashed on to the floor, giggling and knocking stools about, looping and writhing like landed fish.

Pinocchio the cat fled.

Bridgie squirted them with water from the sink.

'Ouch, you rat!'

Panting and beaming at each other in high good humour, the boys scrambled to their feet.

'Right, Bridgie . . .'

They closed in for the kill.

'That's enough. Put those stools straight and put your mugs up to be washed.' Their mother had appeared behind them. 'Has anyone made us a drink?'

'Yours is over there; Dad's had his.'

'Thanks. Any volunteers to take the dog out?'

'Homework.' Hal and Bridgie spoke as one.

'Matt?' Mum glanced out of the window; the sky was a dirty yellow-grey.

'In a bit. I'm going to do my bedroom first.'

'What a saint. Good fellow – but I shouldn't leave it too late; it's going to get colder before the day's out.'

*

Matt pottered about in his bedroom, aimlessly moving things here and there. He had a tape on full blast, and idly wagged his head to the beat, whistling half-heartedly. There was a thump on his bedroom floor.

'OK,' he yelled. He turned the volume down. '*Hold me, hold me, you never hold me . . .*' he crooned. '*Hold me, hold me, I'm so cold; we . . .*'

Matt, too, looked out of the window. The sky was evil-looking. Why was the old lady there? Was she still there? Should he *do* something? Tell anybody? But she had trusted him not to. Trusted *him*. She had asked him not to tell, tried to make him promise. She had run away, like he was going to. Had been going to. He wasn't so sure now; he didn't actually feel very sure of anything.

That 'hypo' thing . . . It worried him. How could he find out more about it? Would his old lady die?

He began to plan for the afternoon. He wouldn't be able to go to the barn before then, because of Sunday lunch; roast pork and stuffing and roast potatoes this week. Great. And apple crumble. Pity he couldn't take some hot lunch to the granny. Wonder what her name is – Brown? White? Smith? Jones? He gave a sudden chuckle; granny Smith. Granny Smith! 'Get it?' he asked the unseen audience, 'Get it? Granny Smith apples!' He grinned again to himself at his own joke. But it wasn't funny; Granny Apple must be wondering where he had got to, or maybe she didn't expect him to come. Maybe she just didn't think about it at all, didn't remember him from one day to the next. How long was she going to stay at the barn? It was useless asking questions; she just rambled, and he never understood the answers.

What was he going to do with her?

Matt put another tape on and inked in a Range Rover brochure while he considered.

What did he actually know about her? He ticked off the points in his mind. One: she was an old lady. Two:

she was wearing a tatty pink dressing-gown (with holes in) and filthy fluffy slippers. Three: she called him Charlie. Four: she kept on about a bear. Five: she couldn't keep her head still. Six . . . but he couldn't think of a six. He worked through the points in his mind again. Nothing; there was nothing there to help anybody. No clue.

Why was she running away? What from? It couldn't be from this Charlie person; she seemed to like him (or her; maybe it was short for Charlotte?). Maybe 'they' were going to put her in an Old People's Home and she didn't want to go. Why didn't old people like Old People's Homes? You'd think they would like to be with all their old mates. But she had no luggage. Nobody but an idiot runs away in a dressing-gown and slippers, with no luggage; it's stupid. Was she stupid? Mad? That's it. She had escaped from a Mental Home, climbed down the drainpipe . . . Matt shook his head. There was no way Granny Apple could shin up and down drainpipes; she could only just walk. She shook like a leaf most of the time. The door, then. She had used the door. But surely at night – presumably she had legged it at night if she only had her dressing-gown and slippers on? – surely the doors would be locked at night in a Mental Home? Wouldn't they? And what about the bear? Well, if she were a nutter that took care of the bear. But somehow Matt didn't think of her as a nutter; confused or forgetful, maybe, but not mad.

He worked on with his pen, carefully outlining the bumpers and blocking in black shadows; he would love a Range Rover. It would be really great. He could track over the fields, the stream, even take Granny Apple for a ride!

What was the time? He chucked his pen down and flicked his radio cassette over to the news: '. . . *is still missing. Police are asking anyone who may have seen a person or*

43

persons acting in a suspicious manner or who think they may have useful information to contact . . .'

Matt's pen rolled off on to the floor. He stooped to pick it up and clouted his head on the open drawer.

'. . . and now for the weather we may expect in the Midlands today. The present cold spell will continue well into the coming week, with prolonged outbreaks of heavy snow in most areas and very severe frosts at night. The temperatures are expected to fall to as low as minus fifteen degrees celsius in some areas and high winds are likely to cause some drifting. The cold front is moving . . .'

Matt flicked back to his tape. Snow! Actual snow! Great stuff. When? When would it start snowing?

Giving his head a cursory rub, he shoved back his chair, burst out of the room, and clattered down the stairs.

'Mum, where's Dad?'

'In the stable, I think; do you . . .'

'Good.'

Matt shot out of the door, banged it to, and raced out to find his father.

'Dad, Dad! It's going to snow!'

'Could do. It's cold enough.'

'It's *going* to; it said so. On the news.'

'Much?'

'Drifting, they said . . . Dad, where's my sledge?'

'You won't want it yet.'

'Yes, I will; I do. Where is it?'

'Up in the loft, I should think, but . . .'

'Thanks.'

Matt was off, speeding along the path back to the cottage.

'Matt . . .'

'Not now, Mum. I'm getting my sledge down.'

'What about the dog?'

'Hang *on*. Shan't be a sec.'

Minutes later, Matt emerged triumphant – cob-webbed, and clutching his polypropylene skimmer.

'Matt, it hasn't even *started* to snow yet. Take that thing out of the kitchen and take Bodger round a field or two. You can take him out properly this afternoon, unless the weather turns too nasty.'

'Yeh, OK. Come on, Bodge. Bodge? Bodge, it's going to snow!'

They roared out, mad as hatters. Snow. It was going to snow.

CHAPTER SEVEN

What on earth was Matt doing? From the top of the opposite bank Guppy paused, puzzled; Matt and Bodger were scampering along beside the stream, jumping over the squelchy bits.

'Hurry up, Bodge!' Matt's clear voice floated out on the cold air. Bodger had stopped for a bit of private investigation into water rats, ramming his nose into promising-looking holes and snorting with excitement. He began to dig, clawing at the grass roots, spraying his belly with damp earth . . .

'Bodger, come *on*! We haven't got time . . .'

Guppy slipped and skidded down through the tangled undergrowth, his fishing-bag rolling and bumping behind him.

'Matt! Hi, Matt! 's me . . . Matt!'

Had he heard? He did seem to glance up, hesitate; but he didn't stop. Bodger left the water rats and followed him.

46

'Matt!'

No response.

Guppy put his fingers in his mouth and let fly with an ear-splitting whistle. He grinned. He would have to hear that.

Yes, he would. Matt sighed. There was no way he could pretend he didn't know who that was.

Gareth Urquhart Pilbeam hitched himself on to the trunk of a fallen willow and waited for him. He rubbed his freckled nose and settled his hat more firmly on his mop of tangled curls. Could you call it a hat? Matt was never sure. Once it had been a camouflage-cloth army hat, but now it looked as if it had spent years rolling in and out of cow muck and sump oil, being imperfectly washed, and dried by being sat on by an elephant. Except at school, Guppy was never seen without it. Guppy was the nearest thing Matt had to a best friend.

Matt grinned. Fancy a vicar calling his son Gareth Urquhart Pilbeam – fancy giving anyone such a ghastly name. You'd have to be barmy ... although, to be fair, Matt quite liked The Vapouriser, this being the title by which his affectionate and irrepressible family addressed their father.

'Vicar, Vick ... get it?' had said Guppy; that was years ago, when he had first come to the village. 'Plus he's bound to get up people's noses, some people's noses; he's always pushing pews around, and altars. He brought a donkey into church once and it ate the organist's hat. It was great!'

Guppy's nickname was more obvious; firstly because of his initials and secondly because he was dead nuts on fishing, any weather, any time. Like now, for instance.

'Hi, deaf-aid. Didn't you hear me?'

Guppy jumped down from his perch.

'Coming eeling?'

47

'Well ...' Matt dug his hands into his pockets and hunched his shoulders. He kicked idly at a curl of loose bark. 'I ... um ...' What on earth could he say?

Guppy eyed him gravely.

'You going somewhere?'

Matt looked at him; looked away.

'What's up?' And then, 'Why've you got a rucksack? What's in it?'

'I ...' Matt floundered. 'Just things.'

'What things? Tell us ...'

'I will tell you, only ...' Oh gosh, I can't. Matt was desperate. What could he say? Inspiration came. '... only Bridgie says it's to be a secret. From Mum. You mustn't tell Mum.'

'Tell her what?' Guppy was mystified.

'Well, it's her birthday soon and Bridgie and Dad are going to make a sundial and they want lots of big, smooth cobbles to go round the base – in concrete – you know; and little plants in between ...' Matt was warming to his theme.

'Stones? Stones?' Guppy couldn't believe his ears. 'You're spending Sunday afternoon picking up stones? For Bridgie? You must be crackers. Why can't Bridgie get them?'

'Well ...' Why? It was a good point. 'I was taking the dog out anyway, so I said I'd look at the same time.'

'Here?'

'Well, not exactly *here*. There's a ploughed field ...'

'OK, I'll come. How many d'you want? Let's see how many you've got.'

'Oh no, it's ... I've probably got enough to carry for this trip. I'm just taking Bodge a bit further, that's all. He's hardly been out today.'

'Eeling, then?'

'Not with Bodger; he's such a pain.'

That was true; nobody wants a dog when they're

fishing. Guppy gave up.

'See you, then.'

'See you – bet you miss the bus again tomorrow!'

'Hope so! The pitch'll be frozen and we'll have to go on cross-country; I *hate* cross-country . . .'

'Yeh. See you.'

Matt and Bodger set off once more, upstream.

Guppy watched them go, a strangely thoughtful look in his eye. Then he bent, picked up his bag and gear, rammed his hat more firmly down on his head and turned away. Downstream.

It was a close shave. Matt hadn't given Guppy a thought all weekend. It was strange; he seemed to be totally obsessed with Granny Apple. Glancing at his watch, he broke into a run. A few specks of snow began to fall.

Arriving at the barn, all seemed much as before. No sign of life, no disturbance that he could see. All quiet. Easing the heavy door towards him a little, he and Bodger slipped through into the musty darkness, barely able to see after the dim light outside. It was very still. Little puffs of dust stirred around his feet as he walked, and Bodger sneezed; soon he disappeared behind a pile of old machinery. It was damp, cold, and Matt shivered. The high windows framed dull blocks of brooding, pewter-coloured sky; flecks and flurries of snow drifted thinly across the openings, blew gently in to settle and melt slowly on the dirty stone floor.

Matt glanced across to where he had left Granny Apple sleeping the night before. He saw the humped shape of the blankets in the dimness; she didn't stir.

Oh well, all the better. He wouldn't waken her. She could come to no harm asleep, and he would do what he had to do first.

Matt took off his rucksack, quietly, and set about lighting

49

a fire. Carefully he made his little wigwam of straw, fed it with little strips of an old woven basket, propped up against that a few twigs and odds and ends, and finally laid on some broken lengths from an old hayrick. The fire was alight, drawing well; warm and cheerful and delightfully friendly. Shadows flickered and danced, played hide-and-seek over the bales and the old tack, sent snakes of shadow flickering up the walls behind the hanging ropes and cobwebs. Tongues of flame licked up and the dirty lime-washed walls flowered with gold and apricot and rose. Matt stood back, quite still for once, absorbed in this unexpected beauty. His over-stretched mind felt strangely comforted.

There was a sharp crack; a tiny, glowing ember shot out and landed by his foot, boring a neat hole in the thread of straw. A broom. Matt looked around; he needed a broom. He moved off into the shadows, rummaging about among the old pails and broken tools. What could he use? Finally, he found an old pitchfork, one prong snapped off short, and managed to wrap a bundle of sacking round it. Bringing it back to the fire, he began to sweep the surrounding stone floor clear of dirt and rubbish, a wide clean circle. His mother would have been proud of him! Matt chuckled to himself, remembering the many arguments over clearing up his bedroom. Oh well; now for the food.

Out of his rucksack he drew a rolled-up towel and felt it anxiously. Good; still OK. Carefully, he took from it two foil parcels and set them on the embers at the edge of the hearth. He stood the vacuum flask to one side, opened a packet of soup powder and poured it into his enamel camping mug, ready. Next came two polythene bowls, cutlery, containers. Should he waken her yet?

No need, it would all keep hot for a few minutes. He would go and see what he could find in the way of wood. A cautious snap of his fingers brought Bodger bounding up, anxious to help, and together they slipped outside and began to search.

It wasn't difficult. In a few minutes they had made quite a pile (or rather Matt had; Bodger only supervised): branches, old fencing, broken packing cases, even a rotting doormat they had dragged from the cottage porch. The snow wasn't really lying yet, but none the less they were more than ready to go back to the fire.

Matt peeled off his wet gloves and draped them over an old pail by the fire, where they began to steam gently. They had kept his hands clean, he supposed – well, fairly.

Now; it was time to waken Granny Apple. Sunday lunch for drop-outs was now being served. Come on, Granny Apple!

Matt bent over the 'day-bed'. 'Wake up,' he called gently, 'wake up!'

Then, not so gently, urgently, 'Hey, wake up; don't you . . .'

His hand, drawing back the blankets, stopped, faltered. The snug cocoon that had held the little old lady was hollow, empty. Matt put a suddenly shaking hand inside. It was cold.

Granny Apple had gone.

CHAPTER EIGHT

Slowly, Matt straightened up. He looked at his hand as if it could tell him something. Nothing. It could tell him nothing. He stood, still as death; unable to think, numb...

After a while he became aware of some pressure on his foot, a warmth against his leg, an insistent sound scratching at his mind.

What was going on? Bodger stopped treading on Matt's foot, backed off a little, taut and anxious. Lifting his head, he gave two or three short, sharp yelps, his tail stiff with fear. His eyes were fixed on Matt's white face. What was going on? Why didn't he move? Bodger began to whimper...

With an effort, Matt responded to the dog's need.

'It's OK, Bodge; it's...'

It needed no more. Bodger hurled himself upon Matt

who, losing his balance, toppled sideways on to the heap of blankets. Bodger clambered all over him, licking any part he could reach in an ecstasy of relief.

'Bodge, shurrup! Stop it, Bodge; I don't want licking. Gerroff, you biff!' and then, with a sudden change of mood, Matt flung his arms around the excited Bodger and buried his head in his neck. 'Bodger ...' Matt's shoulders were shaking. 'Oh, Bodge...'

For a few moments, boy and dog lay together, the warm furry body solid and comforting; steadying...

But it wasn't desperately easy to breathe and soon Bodger began to struggle out from under. Anyway, he wasn't allowed on beds and was beginning to feel guilty. Giving Matt's ear a passing lick from a pink tongue, he climbed down rather furtively, shook himself and ambled off to settle down in front of the fire. He yawned a couple of times and then, unhurriedly, rolled on to his side, stretched, and with a grunt of contentment folded himself for sleep.

Matt envied him. He thought he would never sleep again. From being stunned, his mind had woken into a jumble of frenzied, whirling thoughts. He didn't seem able to complete any of them; they battered against his panic like trapped birds...

Think, he told himself, think. Lying back, his hands locked behind his head, he stared up into the high, shadowed vault of the roof. Huge beams crossed from wall to wall like bridges; smoked, rough-hewn rafters stretched up to meet each other at the upper edge of darkness; soft swags and nets of dirt-encrusted cobwebs swayed a little in the seeking winds; and two thin sparrows quarrelled, tugging at a scrap of white down ... Matt shut his eyes. He must think. He hadn't expected this; everything else, but not this. Yet, after all, why should he have supposed that Granny Apple would stay, would wait for him? Had he said he would come back? Had he? Was it *his* fault if . . . if she . . . But his mind refused to follow this thought. There was something he ought to do; somewhere he ought to go; some new danger . . .

Suddenly Matt jerked upright. What was it? Asleep – he'd been asleep, for heaven's sake! How could he have . . . There it was again. Two soft, scraping, rubbing noises. Silence. Then two more. Silence. Two more . . . Matt's eyes widened; he screwed his head round towards the door, gasped, and then, weakly, 'Oh, it's you.'

Bodger lifted his head, thumped his tail a couple of times in a feeble sort of way, but didn't bother to stir himself further.

Granny Apple stood there against the light, tiny, frail, and sprinkled with snow.

'Hello, dear.'

Shuffling forward, two shaky steps at a time, she made her way in. The fire had burned low now, only a few flames trembled at the edges of the glowing embers; the melting snow on her draggled slippers winked and sparkled with reflected light; small wet footprints followed her; two or three drops ran together and slid from the hem of her dressing-gown . . . She was so wet. Where had she been?

'Granny Apple, you're sodden. Where have you been? It's snowing outside; you shouldn't go out in this . . .'

'But I have to, dear. I have to.'

Why on earth?

'Why do you have to? It's too cold for you. Promise me you won't go out again. Promise, Granny Ap . . .' Matt bit his tongue.

But '. . . apple? Apples?' She smiled. 'I was looking for a bush. There are no leaves on . . .' (Of course not, not this early in the year; she must be bonkers. Poor old

54

Granny Apple.) '. . . no leaves at all. I had to go quite a long way to find what I was looking for . . .'

'But what *were* you looking for? Why do you want a . . . bush, was it?' (Or did she mean 'bear'?)

'But, dear, a lady has to be private.'

'Has to be pr . . .? Oh. Oh, I see. I . . . er . . .' and poor Matt wished that the floor would open up and swallow him. His face glowed scarlet with embarrassment and his ears flamed, hot with distress. Of course. What a simple explanation – and to think how he had panicked, worried himself sick that she had run away again. Or died; or . . . but he wouldn't think of that.

After what seemed a lifetime, he dared to look at her again and had the surprise of his life. She was grinning at him, actually grinning, with a gleam of pure mischief in her eye!

'Granny Apple, you're a wicked old lady!' chortled Matt.

'I know,' she agreed, quite unabashed, sane and sensible. 'I always was.'

And they both fell about with shrieks of laughter.

Finally, 'Oh, I feel . . . oh, I don't know how I feel.' Granny Apple wiped her eyes with her wet sleeve and tottered over to sit down, limping a little.

'No!' Matt stopped her. 'No. You'll make the blankets all wet. You must get dry.' Was this going to be embarrassing, too? 'Take your dressing-gown off and wrap up in a blanket. Then we'll dry your things off . . .' and he turned to make up the fire.

She said something, protesting. He didn't catch what. Busily, he built up the wood, watching the flames grow as the branches hissed and oozed sticky cream sap. Two woodlice clambered frantically away from the heat, teetered over the edge and . . . but Matt caught them just in time, set them down gently and watched them lumber off into the shadows.

'Good boy; good . . . they're safely away now.'

Granny Apple stood behind him, swaying a little, nodding her little head wisely. She seemed bright, alert. Too bright, perhaps?

'You hungry?' Matt pulled forward the two foil parcels, still warm.

'Well, yes, but . . .' She backed away a little. Then, 'Yes, I would like . . . something. I . . .'

'OK. Coming up!'

Matt raked forward an old chair. It had no back, and one of the rungs had gone, but it seemed firm enough. He coaxed her forward, slowly.

'Sit down; dinner is served.'

It was a delight to watch her. Squatting by the hearth, keeping a careful eye on the dressing-gown and slippers that were slowly drying out, steaming and sometimes smelling a bit singed in the fierce heat, Matt was happy to the depths of his soul. *He* had done it all; *he*, the useless one; *he* had organized a meal fit for kings – hot, good and filling. He chose not to dwell on the fact that he had filched various items from home, or even that the cooking he had done was pretty basic: any fool could bung a spud in the Rayburn. He drifted off into a day-dream – he would run a café when he was older; he would call it 'The Granny Apple' and every Sunday he would have a special menu. He could see it now, printed out on bright green card, cut into the shape of an apple: tomato soup; jacket potatoes filled with butter and grated cheese; apple crumble and fresh cream; coffee. Wine extra. (Did you put 'Wine extra'? He wasn't sure . . .)

'Is there any sugar?'

He came to with a start. Sugar? He had forgotten the sugar! No, he hadn't. Turnip-head. There was some in the stuff he had brought yesterday.

56

'Hang on, Granny. Shan't be a sec.'

Rummaging about in the polythene bags, he found the sugar – and something else.

'Hey, Granny, look at this! Look what I've found . . .'

'. . . and did you say coffee, dear?'

'Yes.' Regretfully, Matt put down his trophy. Carefully unscrewing the vacuum flask, he put a coffee-bag in the lid and poured on the water. Was it still hot enough? He had already used some for the soup. Yes, it seemed to be OK. Milk. Milk? Oh, yes, He went off, came back with a tin of evaporated milk, spiked two holes in the top, and poured a thin, rich stream into the cup.

'How much sugar do you like?'

Granny Apple was slowly savouring the warm but oddly sticky-looking crumble out of one of the foil parcels. She was probably right to sprinkle it with sugar; it did make it look a bit better.

'Just one, dear, please.'

He spooned it in and stirred it well; set it down by her feet. Old people's feet weren't very pretty, Matt decided. He gave an involuntary shiver.

'What have you found, love?' She set down the crumble. She had only eaten a little.

'Don't you want any more?' Come to think of it, she hadn't made a brilliant job of her potato; perhaps it was too difficult for her to manage. But she had done her best, and she had had all the soup.

'No, dear. It was lovely, but I've had enough now.' She sipped her coffee slowly, wrinkling her nose at the odd taste of the tinned milk but grateful for the warmth.

'What is it you've found?'

'These!' Triumphant, Matt produced a pack of playing-cards. 'Want a game?'

It was a lovely afternoon. They sat there, wrapped in warmth, lit by the flickering firelight, crouched over their cards. Their eyes sparkled; their fingers hovered, selecting; their mouths tightened with concentration. Two-handed whist, beat your neighbour, gin rummy . . . They hardly spoke, but they were friends, partners. The lift of an eyebrow, a sideways glance, a sudden jerk of the shoulder, sent them into gleeful chuckles; victory, defeat, it was all one to them. This was their only world.

That would have been the time to slip in the questions, to lead the old lady on to talk, to reminisce; but Matt never even thought of it. He was too happy, too . . . I don't know what I was, thought Matt. She liked me; she liked *me*. Running along beside the stream, he broke into a few wild cavortings of pure joy. But it couldn't last.

'What shall I do?' Matt hardly realized he was speaking aloud. It was awful. Granny Apple had been trying a hand of patience. Matt had straightened her bed; he had put some sandwiches and some squash and a cup all ready for her, for later; and then he had tidied round the fire. He had brushed it up (or rather pitchfork-sacked it up); pulled their straw-bale table back to the stack; helped Granny Apple back into her dressing-gown. As she raised her left arm to push it into the waiting sleeve, her nightgown, torn down the side, sagged away from her body and disclosed the most appalling wound – he supposed it was a wound – across her left thigh. Six inches or more long, it was wide and raw, weeping and revolting; puckered, crusted round the edges, it made Matt's stomach turn over.

'Granny!' It was almost a shriek. 'Granny, what have you *done*? What's happened to you?'

'Hmm?'

'Your leg; you're hurt. You . . .' and then the fire cracked, a flame spluttered bright against the dark. Gingerly Matt turned her round to the light, gently lifted the torn cloth, tried to see more clearly.

But, 'Don't – oh, please don't. Please . . . leave me. I

58

shouldn't have ... And you ...' Granny Apple had gone. In her place was a pathetic, crumpled child, bewildered, lost; terrified of Matt's intentions. 'No, no. Go away. Please. I was only ... looking ... I ...' and she began to sob, helplessly, and beat at Matt with her tiny hands as he steered her to the bed, laid her down and began to lap her in the blankets, the covers. 'I ... they told me not to, but ... it was the bear. And I can't ...'

'You need help.' It was all becoming too much for Matt. He would have to ...

'No.' She shook and twisted under his hands. 'No, no, no.' Tears coursed down her thin cheeks; her pale eyes held his. 'No. No one must know. They'll ...' She didn't finish, but she was plainly terrified. 'You mustn't tell anyone. You'll help me. I don't want anyone else. I don't want anyone ...'

Matt tripped over a tussock of grass. Where was Bodger? Chasing rabbits? He stopped; called and whistled ... and while he waited, all he could see was that appalling wound.

CHAPTER NINE

'Bring that bowl a bit nearer, will you?'

Matt watched anxiously as his mother bathed Bodger with warm water. The cut on his belly was only an inch or so long, if that, but crusted with mud.

'What on earth was he doing? Didn't you see him?'

'I think he was off after a rabbit.'

'Matt, if you take him out you do have to keep an eye on him – there are sheep in lamb all over the place.'

'He doesn't chase sheep.'

'No, maybe not; but a farmer may not wait to find out.'

'But that's not fair!'

'Life isn't fair . . .'

Matt seemed preoccupied, worried. His mother looked at him thoughtfully.

'What's biting you?'

'Huh?'

'What's bothering you? You're like a bear with a sore head.'

Why was everyone so obsessed with bears? First

Granny Apple, now his mum.

'It's always my fault . . .'

His mother didn't say anything.

'Well, I couldn't help it . . . Is he going to be all right?'

'He'll be OK. Sprinkle some of that powder over the cut.'

'What's it for?'

'It's antiseptic. Doesn't taste very nice, either. Maybe it'll stop Bodger licking himself into even more of a mess.'

'But won't cuts heal by themselves?'

'Depends; they can get infected, go bad, sort of; poison the whole system.'

'Often?' This was alarming. 'Do they often?'

'Sometimes, if the animal is ill or old. They can't fight infection so well. Don't look so worried,' she ruffled his hair, 'Bodger's quite a young dog, fit as a flea; he'll be fine. He could have licked it clean himself, I expect, but it might have been barbed wire – and that's nasty. When it's rusty it's best to be careful.'

Matt shivered.

'Don't worry; he'll be OK.' And then, as Matt said nothing, 'Go on; get yourself sorted out for school tomorrow – your games kit is on a chair in the other room and I think Dad's put your dinner-money on your desk. Then you can wash your hands and we'll have tea.'

She began to clear up, rolling the dirty swabs in newspaper, emptying the bowl.

'No, Bodge; Bodger! Leave it alone . . . Bridgie, come and feed the dog, will you? It'll take his mind off his tum; well,' she laughed, 'maybe not.'

The powder was bright blue, but it said that it was for veterinary use only so it was no good for the old lady. It was 'anti-larval', too; anti-larval? What on earth was that? Anyway, it was no good. He couldn't use it. Matt had had a quick look on his way to bed.

What else could he use? Wounds had to be kept clean, his mum said; and Granny Apple ... Matt shuddered again at the very thought of that leg. It was horrible. Well, he would just have to take some stuff out of the first-aid box, TCP or something. Did it have to be mixed with water? He didn't know. What else should he take? He thought about Bodger. Cotton wool, hot water, some cloth – that woolly-looking stuff that was fluffy on one side; lint, was it? – some sticky tape; scissors, he mustn't forget scissors ... What else?

Matt was worried. It was all getting completely out of hand. It was all very well for Granny Apple to say he mustn't tell anyone; OK, she was frightened – heaven knows what of – but where did that leave him? What if anything happened to her? Was that going to be his fault, too?

'It's not my fault,' Matt muttered angrily to himself. 'It's not. She's making me keep quiet; and anyway ...' – anyway he was already in it up to his neck, whatever 'it' was. He'd lied to his father (well, sort of lied) about going out at night; he had taken food; he had dodged round Guppy ... where was it all going to end?

Matt groaned and gave his pillow a despairing thump, sat down heavily on the bed ... and on his Airfix plane. Savagely, he hurled the wreck across the room at his waste-paper bin.

'Matt? What on earth are you doing? You're supposed to be in that bath by now. Hurry up – other people want to use the bathroom.'

I bet they do, thought Matt bitterly. Nice clean little lives, no problems. They even liked their dear little schools.

Scowling, he scuffed through to turn on the taps.

Twenty minutes later, his cassette going full blast from his bedroom, he lay in the steam and the hot water, idly

62

trying to pick up the nail-brush with his foot. Relaxed now and warm, he felt better. OK, so he had problems. But he could sort them out, of course he could. He wasn't a complete 'remmy'; he'd show them.

So. Problems. He lay back and looked at them in his mind. There was the wound. Well, he would take what stuff he could tomorrow and, clean it up. Try to. Tomorrow? He groaned. It was school tomorrow. Should he cut school, doss off? Some of the kids did, but . . . He would be jolly cold; it was snowing again and the wind was icy. No hockey, anyway; that was one good thing. Cross-country instead, worse luck. Cross-country? That was an idea . . . Yes!

His foot thwacked down on to the nail-brush. A plume of soapy water leapt up, collapsed over the floor, just missing his pyjamas.

That's it. He would nip off during the cross-country to the corner shop, buy some tea-bags and bread, maybe some sausages and beans, other bits and pieces, cut across Agnew's meadows and dump the stuff ready to collect later. He could take it along to Granny Apple after school. Easy; he could join the run again and finish with the others – the stragglers, anyway. Brilliant.

Was there a snag?

He lowered his chin into the water; he started blowing bubbles but they went up his nose . . .

'Matt, hurry up. You've been in there for hours. Surely you're clean by now?'

'Nearly. Just doing my neck.'

He hadn't started washing. Where was the soap? After a lot of splashing and stirring and the odd tidal wave, he found it; it looked rather like a dying jelly-fish, shiny and soft. It oozed between his fingers. Oh, well . . . There was a snag. He didn't know if he had enough money. He'd have to buy bread. Tea-bags, too – he would have to buy tea-bags; he wasn't going to mess about with tea-leaves

63

and a tea-pot, and anyway he hadn't got one. She could have coffee, he supposed, but . . . No, his old lady had asked for tea and she should have tea. She would drink more if she liked it and that would keep her warmer.

The blind wasn't drawn down and Matt could see a little topping of snow on the bottom ledges of the frosted panes. The blind-cord danced and tapped; the wind whined in the overflow. Would Granny Apple be warm enough until he got there? Would she go out in the snow again? Matt blushed. She would have to. But she had got straw all round her bed, and blankets and things, and sacks. She could keep the fire going. He had left plenty of wood. And food, 'but it's cold,' Matt worried. 'Cold food, cold drink . . .and it's really bitter out there . . .'

Drifting, they had said, and minus fifteen degrees – was that cold? How cold? Hypo . . . hypo-something: a killer, Hal said. Hal knew; Hal knew most things. Wonder what it's like to be brainy, Matt wondered, having to work all the time. Oh well, it wasn't likely to bother him. He sighed.

'Matt . . .'

'OK. I'm just getting out.'

He yanked out the plug, dangled it round the tap. The water seemed to be a funny colour; was he really that dirty? No, couldn't be. Must be the dye out of the flannel, or the soap, or . . .

'Don't forget to clean the bath!'

'OK, give us a chance.' Matt attacked the tide-line with the scrubber, perfunctorily, and dumped it back on the corner of the bath to dribble into the escaping flow. He shivered. It was freezing. Clambering out, he seized his towel, kicked the mat back to the washbasin and scampered back to his bedroom. A trail of flat, wet footprints followed him.

He changed his tape, switched on the fire, rubbed at his hair and pondered. Money – he had to have money, just in case. He put what he had into his pencil-case.

'I'll borrow some; only a little. Borrowing is all right. It's for Granny Apple.'

Matt crept silently along the landing, into his parents' bedroom.

CHAPTER TEN

'Hello, Matt; don't often see you in here. Do you want any help?'

Matt swung round, startled, a book in one hand and two or three others slipping about in the crook of his other arm.

It was Monday, lunch break. In the school library several heads turned for a moment and then the quiet hum and rustle started up again.

'What's all this? First-aid? *How the Body Works*. Scouts, is it? Got a badge to do?'

Old Fungus looked down, a little puzzled by Matt's flustered face.

'N-no, Sir, it's ... Well, I wanted to look at something.' Matt was obviously ill at ease.

'Anything special?' Mr Stephenson stroked his beard thoughtfully. Then, 'Come on. Put the books down here

66

and let's see what we can find. What was it you wanted to look up?'

'Nothing. I mean ... well, it's sort of ... private.' Matt shifted uneasily from foot to foot. Now what was he to do? Why did old Fungus have to stick his nose in ?

Private? Nothing? Mr Stephenson sat down. He smiled encouragingly.

No response except a nervous scowl.

How old was Matt? Twelve? Thirteen? Mr Stephenson clasped his hands together on the table before him and spoke even more gently.

'Sit down, Matt. Now, what's your problem? Is there something you don't understand? Can I help? You look a pretty normal sort of scrub to me!' His eyes twinkled mischievously.

'Me?' Oh, gosh, old Fungus was going to tell him about the birds and the bees and all that rot! Matt squirmed. 'It's not *me*.' But he didn't explain any further; how could he?

'Your family? Everything OK, is it?'

'Yes ...' Gosh, this was awful! '... er, Sir,' Matt added, as an afterthought.

Not the family then. But something.

'Can you manage to find what you're looking for? Do you need any help?"

'Yes, thanks. I think so, except ... Sir, how do you spell hypo ... hypo ... hype ... being cold, Sir?'

Matt's eyes were anxious.

'Hypothermia?' Hypothermia? What on earth was the lad on about ... 'Hypothermia? Want the school heating turned up, do you? You should eat more breakfast if you want to keep warm, young Matthew!'

Fungus grinned. Matt achieved a weak smile in response and wondered how to explain his sudden interest in an unheard-of medical condition.

*

He didn't have to explain; Guppy, thank goodness, stuck his nose in. Having run Matt to earth in, of all unlikely places, the library, having found him surrounded by what he loosely termed 'body books', Master Pilbeam proceeded to take the Michael.

'Tell him, Sir – it was a stork, wasn't it, Sir! Fancy a stork bothering to get beak-strain delivering brain-box here. I bet he picked up the wrong bundle; bet Matt was on the reject pile, due to be recycled ...'

'Gareth, how do you spell "hypothermia"?'

'Hypo ... hypo-what, Sir?'

'Hypothermia.'

'Never heard of it, Sir.'

'Hmm; I'm not surprised. How your father came to take delivery, whether by stork or gooseberry bush, of a son such as you I cannot understand. It puts the whole theory of guardian angels into considerable doubt.'

Guppy winked incorrigibly at Matt, who stood open-mouthed at this exchange.

'No, I fancy you didn't come by stork, nor were you discovered peacefully snoring under a gooseberry bush. You were no doubt abandoned as a horrible little squawking bundle, red-faced and bald, and left in a stout cardboard box on the vicarage steps. That kind man, your father, took you in.' Old Fungus was warming to his theme, '... yes; the box was marked "Export Only" but, as your father was composing next Sunday's sermon at the time, he failed to follow those extremely explicit instructions. A pity, but there it is. We're stuck with you now for the foreseeable future.

'Now Matthew here,' and old Fungus dumped a heavy paw on Matt's shoulder, 'shows promise; promise. He knows what hypothermia is, don't you?'

'Well, sort of. It's when you get cold and ...'

'You see, Gareth? Try to cultivate an equally useful mind. Acquire wisdom, learning, before it's too late. You can make a start now. Look up "hypothermia" for Matthew; no doubt he wants detailed information in case he should trip over another babe in a cardboard box on a winter's night – though if it's one of your relations, I should advise him to consider very carefully before he decides to save its life.'

'Yes, Sir. Sir, may I ask you something?' Guppy's eyes danced.

'Indeed you may, Gareth; fire away. Anything to dispel the clouds of ignorance, to help you acquire knowledge, however slight.'

'Sir, is it true that you were found in a box labelled "Soft Soap"?'

'No, Gareth, you have been misinformed. My box, as I understand it, carried a clearly written Government Health Warning which cheeky young irks like you would do well to remember.'

Guppy ducked instinctively.

'Yes, Sir.'

It was the afternoon.

Matt grinned appreciatively, and forgot for a moment his ice-cold fingers and the discomfort of the heavy plastic bag banging against his knee as he ran. Not a bad bloke really, old Fungus – so long as you knew when to stop. At any rate, thanks to Guppy, he now knew all about hypothermia (he permitted himself a pleased smirk at remembering the word). But it was worrying; this dying of cold seemed a real danger, and what could he do?

Well, he was doing his best. Peeling off from the run hadn't been as difficult as he had thought it would be. A pause to do up his shoe-lace while the main pack overtook him, a quick check over his shoulder, and then a sudden whisk round the corner of the Red Lion, into the alley and straight over the water-meadows into the shop. He had never been in before. No one knew him.

It hadn't taken long to bag up his purchases and pay for them. Then, after a cautious look out of the door, he had sprinted behind a row of old terraced houses, cut down into the waste ground, raced along the short cut by the stream, and was now nearing the barn from the other side.

No smoke. Matt paused, uncertainly. Had he time to go in? No, he couldn't risk it; his watch was back at school in the 'booty box', locked up for safety in Mr Allen's room. Probably he was ahead of the run, but he didn't know for certain. He must push on to the stile where he planned to rejoin the others, but . . .

'Oh, Granny Apple, you are a bother!' In his anxiety Matt spoke aloud, then clapped a hand over his mouth, suddenly alarmed. But there was no one to hear him.

He ran on.

Once at the barn, he looked for a handy place to hide his bag. Finally he thrust it among some rubbish in the angle of two crumbling walls. The relief! He stretched his cramped fingers, opened and closed them, and then, balling both hands together, blew on them in an effort to warm them up. The wet hem of his PE shorts had chafed his thigh where the bag had swung against him; putting warm spit on it didn't help for long.

Somewhat rested, he stood quite still for a moment and listened. Nothing. Only the faint sound of a tractor very far away and the slightest whisper of a leaf drifting across the hard ground. The barn was wrapped in silence. The blind windows told him nothing. Should he go in? No. He simply must get back to the others. He would come back later, as soon as he was home from school; he and Bodger.

Five minutes later, jogging along beside Guppy, he had little breath to spare for talking.

'Where'd you get to?' Guppy was curious. They

always tried to run together. 'I waited for you but you didn't come.'

No answer.

'Well?'

'Well nothing.' Matt hauled in some more air. 'I bust my lace and then I had to undo it all; and then the knot got jammed ... You needn't laugh – you try it with cold fingers!' Not bad that, on the spur of the moment; Matt was quite pleased with himself.

'I don't think I can feel my toes any more,' Guppy mourned. 'It's cruelty to animals, this is. Is Sir running? Bet he's waiting in a nice warm car somewhere, ready to ferry home the stiffened corpses. I'm going to write to my MP.'

'MP?'

'Member of Parliament, dummy-head.'

'What for? What can he do?'

But Guppy had no more puff for idle conversation and Matt lapsed into his own thoughts.

'Ow!'

Guppy had gone flying. Picking himself up from the frozen track, trying unsuccessfully to lick blood off one elbow and to wipe the snow off his front with the other hand, he stared down at the little body that had tripped him. The eyes were closed, the small head was bent a little sideways, and a thin wind ruffled the delicate feathers on the bird's breast. A hen partridge. Matt picked it up; it weighed nothing. Dead. Carefully he looked it over; there was no mark anywhere, no wound. But dead.

Guppy abandoned his elbow.

'Let's see ...' and after a moment, 'It's the cold. She's just died of cold.' He shivered. 'Come on – before we snuff it, too. I'm perished.'

Matt placed the little hen on the bank, up under the hedge where there was only a thin sprinkling of snow; he smoothed down the feathers on the slight breast with an absent-minded finger. 'Died of cold ... she just died of cold ...' The words circled round his mind, round and round, tighter and tighter ...

He turned to run after Guppy but all he could see was the barn. No smoke. There had been no smoke ... and no sound at all.

Matt was afraid.

CHAPTER ELEVEN

Bodger was the first to arrive at the barn. Running here, running there, yards of pink tongue hanging out, he at least was not cold. He waited happily by the broken gate of the cottage, panting and bright-eyed. Matt came on more slowly, flicking the powdered snow off last year's dead seed heads, watching it whirl about in eddies. A robin sat on a spray of dead bramble, its feathers fluffed out against the biting wind. It piped a thin song.

'Come on, then.' Matt snapped his fingers and Bodger pranced up to him. Struggling with the big door of the barn, Matt opened it a little way. As they went through into the darkness, a fiercer gust slammed it shut behind them.

Gosh, but it was dark. Which way was he facing? Where was Bodger?

'Bodge?' A soft nose pushed at his hand. Then, as his eyes grew used to the dim light, 'Granny? Granny Apple?'

There was no answer.

Bodger and Matt made their way across to the makeshift bed. The old lady lay perfectly still, only her wispy hair showing above the blankets pulled around her, and a tiny hand just visible at the side.

'Granny?' Matt bent over her. ''s me – Matt. Wake up. Wake up, Granny.'

She didn't move. Matt pulled the blanket down a little. 'Granny, wake up ...' Nothing. Was she ... was she dead? Matt's heart knocked against his ribs like a drum. Don't let her be dead!

'Granny!'

Matt began to panic. He pulled the blankets right away, bent down and shook her gently. He could not wake her. He caught his lower lip between his teeth, his eyes misty. Oh, Granny ... He looked at the thin body, curled and shrivelled, quite still. Her clothes were rumpled, dragged up, and the wound showed all too clearly.

Matt felt a little sick.

The flesh around the wound was red and swollen; he put out a cautious finger, drew it back. Pus oozed stickily and the edges were stuck with dirt and fluff. It was very inflamed. It was dreadful. Should ... should he clean it? Should he ... Matt could hardly bear to look at it, let alone ... Oh, come on, he told himself, savagely, come on; you've got to do something. You can't leave it.

He swung the bag from his back. Fumbling a little, he unfastened it and tipped the contents out over the foot of the bed. Cotton wool, watered TCP ... With hands that were not too steady, he began to swab the wound as gently as he could, trying to wipe away the muck. She flinched a little, mumbled, but didn't wake. Oh, Granny ... A tear slid down Matt's cheek; doggedly he went on with his task, gently, carefully, blotting away at the wound, trying to see his mother's hands busy with Bodger's cut. Well, he could not do any more. It was cleaner than it was, and surely the TCP should help, shouldn't it? It must; *please*.

Carefully Matt laid an oblong of clean lint on the wound, strapping it in place with plaster strips, firming them over the swollen area, wincing as he did it. The leg was hot under his hand, hot, and yet Granny Apple was mumbling and shivering, shivering with cold. But at least she was alive. For the moment.

How long ...

Matt pulled himself up; there must be something he could do. She looked terrible, hair all tangled and frizzled. He looked at the odd brown marks down her dressing-gown. What were they? He put his finger through one of the holes; the edge was hard, brittle. There were red patches down her legs, blisters ...

'Where ...? Where am ...? Is it there?' Granny Apple opened her eyes, moved her head from side to side, restless, bewildered.

'It's OK.' Matt pulled up the blankets, tucked them round her shoulders. 'It's OK. You've been asleep, that's all. It's only me.'

'Only you ...' Her eyes began to close, her head stilled. She drifted off to sleep.

It didn't take Matt long to make the fire. Cheerful flames were soon licking up the dark chimney, the wood snapped and settled, a circle of warmth grew.

Bodger and Matt sat together, both gazing into the embers, minds suspended. A pan of baked beans kept warm on one side; the toasting-fork in Matt's hand drooped lower, the impaled sausages swelling in the heat. A drop of fat fell, and there was a sudden sizzle and splutter of flame. Bodger flinched, lifted a wary paw. Matt jerked awake, twisted the sausages round with cautious fingers, shaded his eyes from the heat as he bent forward again. Soon they were done. They smelt wonderful! Toast? No, he would wake Granny Apple first, get her organized. He propped the sausages across the pan handle and went over to the bed.

It was difficult to rouse her. Should he leave her to

sleep? No, surely she should eat. Anyway, after all his efforts to buy the food and his plots to deliver it, she had jolly well better eat it! Matt gave a brief smile, but it was soon gone and it did not reach his eyes. Come on, little Granny, come on ...

By the time he had coaxed and bullied her to sit up, helped her across to the old chair, settled a blanket round her, Matt was beginning to wonder how he was going to make it back home in time for his own evening meal.

He unscrewed the vacuum flask, made her tea, and left her sipping it while he made toast. Watching her, he saw her hands shake, her head weaving. She spilt a little.

'... don't stop me; please ...' She gave a sudden sobbing moan '... I didn't know ... Please ... I ... Charlie? Are you there? ... can't see; I can't see ... and you ...' Her thin voice petered out. She sat quite still, her eyes blind.

She was going mad.

'Granny!' Matt was desperate. 'Granny? You ... Drink your tea. Please ... drink your tea.'

Nothing happened. She did not seem to have heard him. Where was she now?

'Granny ...'

'Hmm?'

She turned her head a little, looked at him.

'Who ... who are you? Who ...'

Who was he?

'I'm Matt. You know I am. Granny ... Here, eat this. Can you eat this ...?' Please let her eat this; please.

'Well, I ...'

Matt cut a piece of sausage, lifted it on a fork to her mouth.

'Come on; it's good. It'll warm you up.'

'Yes. But I ...'

'Come on; open ...'

Obedient as a child, she opened her mouth. Matt

76

popped in the sausage; took a spoonful of beans, a corner of toast . . .

Well, she had had something, he supposed. He raced home so fast that he hardly noticed the cold. Monday; it was Monday now. He could not possibly get to her until after school tomorrow and by then . . . anything could happen.

Matt caught his breath on a sob.

CHAPTER TWELVE

'What's up with Matt?'

It was breakfast-time, Tuesday. Hal was wolfing bacon and sausages, one eye on the clock. Bridgie, toying with a piece of sausage (she hated being made to eat a cooked breakfast), was looking thoughtful.

'Do you know?'

Hal paused, fork half-way to his mouth. He looked puzzled.

'What are you on about?'

'Matt.'

'How d'you mean?'

'He isn't talking.'

Hal considered this. It was true. The noisiest creature of his acquaintance, Matt, and he had eaten his food in dark, abstracted silence and simply melted back upstairs.

'Dunno.'

'What "dun" you know?' Mum had reappeared in the kitchen with the post.

'Matt. He hasn't said a word. Matt; the multi-decibel bacon-brain!'

'Mm ... Something's bothering him. You don't know, either of you?'

'Nope. Hey, is that the time? I'll miss the bus!' Hal gulped down a glass of milk, shoved one arm into his coat, grabbed his scarf and his bag and shot out of the door, banging it behind him.

'Bridgie, has Matt said anything about school?'

'No, not a thing.'

Bridgie drifted off for her coat, came back to ask for 20p, and stood still, considering.

'Bridgie, you have to catch the bus too. Stop dreaming.'

Bridgie was unconcerned.

'Hal will get Bones to wait for me.'

'Bones?'

'The driver.'

'Just move, young lady.'

'OK, OK; I'm going. Bye.'

Clearing the wreckage from the table, their mother sighed, thoughtful.

Then, 'Matt?'

Thumps came from overhead.

'Matt, it's twenty past eight. What about your bus ...'

Drawers were pulled out, slammed in. The bedsprings twanged. Something fell over.

'Mum?'

'Yes?'

'Mum, where've you put my RS file?'

'Where've I ... What would *I* want with your RS file? I expect it's where you left it.'

'Where?'

'I don't know; under the settee, on the side ...'

Matt thundered downstairs, swung into the drawing-room, and emerged clutching assorted books, file included. Shoving them higgledy-piggledy into his old RAF bag, he remarked rather obviously, 'Got them.'

He hooked up his anorak by one sleeve and threw it over his shoulder; with a brief 'See you!', he sauntered out into the snow.

'Matt, put it *on*!'

'It's not cold.'

'Matt, it's freezing; put it on. And don't hang about after school, either.'

'OK.'

He began struggling into his anorak, at the same time sliding his feet like skis. He scooped up a handful of snow and lobbed it at his mum, but she had gone inside.

School was hopeless. His mind simply wouldn't consider latching on, writing facts, listening. It had its own circles to tread, its own plans, its own fears . . .

'Matthew, will you read out your work so far?'

Matt looked at old Fungus, bewildered; then his eyes slid away. She might die . . .

'Matthew.' Mr Stephenson's usually kind face was severe. 'Matthew, have you written *anything*?'

'What . . . what about, Sir?'

The class tittered and then fell awkwardly silent.

'At lunch break, Matthew, you will come to my room and spend some time finding out, the hard way, and you will take some extra work home to be done tonight.'

'Tonight?' Matt was horrified. 'But . . . but I can't, Sir, I can't. Not tonight. I . . .'

'Tonight, Matthew . . . and no excuses.'

'But, Sir, it's not excuses. I . . .' What could he say?

'You have a date, perhaps?'

'Yes . . . I mean, no . . . I don't know . . .' Matt flushed; he loosened his collar, it was unaccountably hot.

But out there . . . He looked out at the thin snow, the grey racing clouds, the stark, ragged cold.

'Sir . . .'

'Tonight, Matthew. I'll explain at lunch break. Now

get on with your corrections.'

Everything went wrong. He lost his dinner-money, he spilt paint down his blazer, he broke a chisel in woodwork, and Nibby had a fit on him in maths. And all the while, Granny Apple haunted his mind like pain.

He only managed to escape from the cottage by leaving Bodger behind; Mum wanted him to stay in and start his homework before the others came home, but he simply had to leg it over to the barn while it was still light. He dodged out when she had gone over to the stable for more wood. He hoped she would not miss him with Bodger still in the kitchen, in his bed.

The wind was vicious; his forehead ached with a deep cold as he battled on, head down. As he drew close to the barn, a branch whipped his face and beaded his cheek with blood. He skidded on an ice-filled rut and threw his arms about wildly as he fought to regain his balance. Not much further; oh, to be out of the wind . . .

Granny Apple was alive. Her cheeks were flushed and her eyes, when he finally roused her, were wild and very bright. None of the sandwiches had been touched and the vacuum flask lay on its side, a damp brown stain seeping into the wooden chair. The cup rolled on the floor.

She was strangely talkative, excited even, but she made little sense. Bouts of shivering racked her and yet, as Matt helped her to sit up, her body seemed hot and dry under his hands. Her head bobbed and jerked constantly and her thin hands hovered and plucked at the blankets as if performing some strange ritual dance.

A great fear gathered in the shadows; it gripped Matt's heart with hands of ice.

He hurried to light the fire. The wind howled and whined like a creature crazed; loose straw was lifted by its searching breath and whirled along the floor; old ropes tapped and banged against the walls, and somewhere a chain rattled. What ... what was that noise? It ... no, it was nothing. Nothing. Matt tried to convince himself, but the match he held was not quite steady. It flickered and went out. Fool, fool, there's nothing out there. What could there be?

'. . . the bear; it was in there. I . . .' Granny was sobbing now, sobbing and moaning, struggling up in terror. She raised her arms, shielding her face.

Matt was stiff with horror.

'Charlie tried to stop me, caught hold of me, but someone had to . . .'

There was a screak against the door of the barn, noises in the rising wind. The door opened outwards, it could not be pushed inwards, but . . .

Fire; a bigger fire. Matt needed its comforting glow, its brightness, its strength. He heaped on more dry wood, built it up. Flames began to lick up, the wind roared in the chimney and the heart grew fierce and red.

Again that odd rattle and scrape. Matt stared transfixed at the door. Long moments passed. A sudden fiercer gust ... or was it a snuffle; a creak of wood, a cracking ...

The scream ripped through him, seemed to wrench him apart. But it wasn't him. For a moment Matt wasn't sure. It was Granny Apple, screaming and screaming, high and hopeless, and stumbling blindly to the dark shadowed corner at the back of the barn. She tripped and fell and then, horrible to see, dragged herself moaning and blubbering across the broken bales, the loose straw, and tried to dig herself in.

She could not even crawl properly. She had hurt herself; or perhaps her mind had finally snapped, terror and confusion breaking her. Granny Apple, oh Granny Apple ... Matt scrambled after her, crouched down in the straw and caught hold of one thin little hand, down in the dark.

'Don't, it's all right. It's all right, Granny Apple; it's all right. Oh don't, don't! I can't bear it ...' and suddenly Matt himself put his head down into the crook of his arm, crying from sheer weariness of mind, a too heavy responsibility.

It was the smell he noticed first, acrid and bitter; a strange crackling.

He lifted his head, glanced behind him, blind with his tears. What was that glowing, that fierce, shifting light? 'Oh God ...' It was a prayer.

'Granny!'

He stumbled to his feet, horror-struck.

'Granny!'

Desperately, Matt yanked at her arm. Yanked and yanked.

'Get up; oh, get up! Come *on*!'

He bent and tried to lift the sobbing, shaking bundle of bones, but he was at the wrong angle; with her other hand the old lady clung in terror to the twine around one of the lower bales.

'Leave *go*, Granny, leave *go*! We've got to get out; we've got to get out *now*!'

Matt pulled and pleaded. It was no use. Stark terror gave her the strength to resist his efforts and she was beyond reason. It was no bear that had frightened her, no bear. It was fire.

'We're on fire! It's ... we're on fire; the whole place will go up. It's all ... it's all ...' Matt let go of her and stood still. 'It's all my fault.'

He could not move. He could not even think. He could only watch in a fascination of horror as the flames gathered strength and power, flowed up and over the bales, poured like liquid gold across the 'day-bed', the blankets shrivelling and shrinking like dead skins,

83

overwhelmed in the roaring waves that threw up flecks and ripples of light to catch and flare along the dry pale straw on every side . . .

'I think we should try to get out.'

Who spoke? Matt swung round, startled.

The old lady was sitting in the straw, trying to rise.

'Could you help me, dear? It's really very awkward trying to balance. There seems to be nothing solid underneath.'

Matt stared.

'Could you help me?' and, as Matt seemed stunned, 'Dear, we've very little time. You must try and pull yourself together.'

She coughed. The smoke was thickening; it was unpleasant to breathe.

'Yes. Yes, come on – here, catch hold and I'll pull.'

Released from shock, Matt was restored to action. So, miraculously, was the old lady. She was restored beyond . . . But there was no time to think, no time. The fire roared, it was coming closer. It showered them with sparks and burnt-out threads of straw which fell to grey powder in their hair.

The two stood unsteadily, clutching each other, minds racing.

'The window. There must be a window at this end too.' That was the old lady.

Matt looked up over her shoulder.

'Yes, there is. But it's high, too high for you.'

It loomed above them, a shadowy, shifting slit, stuffed with old sacks.

Something rustled by Matt's feet. A rat?

The bottom of the narrow opening was above Matt's head. He reached up, tugging desperately at the sacks, wrenching them free in clouds of dust and grit that fell into his face, his open mouth. Some went in his eyes. He spat and choked, struggled for breath. There was no purchase for his frenzied hands, moving blind about the brickwork above.

Higher, he must be higher.

The fire roared. The heat grew and the air was thick with smoke.

They began to cough.

Could he move some bales over? Had he time? Pull the old lady up? But the drop the other side. She would fall, fall on her white tangled hair, her soft hair . . .

It was all clear as a photograph in Matt's overwrought mind: he could see the small figure splayed on the snow-drifted rubble, dead, one arm twisted awkwardly beneath the thin body and the tiny head haloed in blood . . .

He could not do it. There was no way out.

'We're trapped.'

CHAPTER THIRTEEN

Hal came home on the early bus. Games had been cancelled.

'Hal, thank goodness.' His mother looked anxious. 'Matt's disappeared to heaven knows where, and now the dog's gone. He must have slipped out when I filled the potato basket. I've called and called; maybe there's a bitch on heat.'

'I know.' Hal heaved a sigh. 'Will I change and will I go and look for him.'

'Well . . .'

'My feet are frozen. I'm not going till I've thawed out.' Hal was adamant. It wasn't fair.

'Look, I'll make you some toast and a cup of tea while you get changed, and warm your socks on the Rayburn if you throw them down. But you must go; it'll be easier to find him while it's still light.'

'OK, if I must.'

Hal threw his bag into the dining-room and draped his anorak over a chair. He went up to his room.

The light was fading as he slid down to the stream. There was no problem in finding the dog. Bodger's trail, once he had picked it up beyond the churchyard, was clearly printed in the snow, together with that of someone who wore wellies just a little smaller than his own. Matt?

What was the idiot up to now . . .

'You must be brave.' Granny Apple's voice was calm.

It was extraordinary. His little old lady, though obviously ill and feverish, shook only with weakness now. There was no trace of fear in her face, none.

What had happened? How come she was making sense? How come . . . Oh no; all at once Matt remembered the Sunday night play. No, please; not that. This guy had been in a coma, freaked out, dying; suddenly he'd sat up, talked perfectly sensibly, and toppled back dead. Dead. It did happen, sometimes, he knew it did; happened just like that. But not to Granny Apple, please not to Granny Apple . . .

Desperately, Matt began lugging bales beneath that high slit, then stopped, sickened by the knowledge that the fall outside would kill her. Water, if only they had water. But what was the use? They would need a lake.

He tripped and fell, landed on the sacks, damp now from the melting snow. The heat was terrifying and they were cool against his cheek; cool . . .

'Granny, quick. Here, wrap these round you, and round your face. They're wet.'

Together they draped themselves in the wet tatters; they smelt vile. They huddled at that high slit.

'Help! Help!'

Matt's voice was a mere croak. What was the use anyway?

Someone put an arm round him, drew his head briefly down and kissed his hair.

'It'll be all right, love; it'll soon be over. Don't fret for me . . . I'm old now.' Her voice was unrecognizable, level

87

and warm.

'But . . .'

'I said don't fret. Matt, is it?'

'Yes, I . . .'

'Matt, I want to thank you. I don't know where I've been or what's been happening – everything's muddled and I don't seem able to remember. But I know you've been with me, looked after me. You're a good boy, Matt; never forget that. Never. Tell them I said so . . .'

'Them?'

'Go on, dear, you must go. There's no time to waste.'

'But I can't leave you; I can't leave you here . . .'

'What else can you do? It's not your fault, none of it's your fault; it was the wind. Now go, Matt; go quickly.'

Tears running down his cheeks, Matt began to say something, desperate, pleading. Then, 'Bodger! It's Bodger!'

Somewhere outside, below the window, there was frenzied, agonized barking. On and on; then a pause and the sound of something slipping and slithering over broken tiles, heartbroken whimpers, short, sharp yelps; and then again that harsh, hollow barking.

Matt clambered up, leaned to look out. The drop was terrifying; he'd never do it.

Bodger went mad. He hurled himself again and again up towards Matt, crashing against the wall, one paw bleeding and agony in every line of him . . .

Hal broke into a run. Bodger, that must be Bodger! And Bodger as he had never heard him, never. Where was he? Was he in a fight? Was he caught? He couldn't be; he sounded . . . Hal didn't know how he sounded, only that it sent a chill of fear right through him. Matt? Was it Matt?

Head down, Hal raced on, slipping, stumbling, his heart pounding and the palms of his hands damp with sweat. Glancing up a moment, he saw wisps of mist rising above Gallows End, curling over the bare trees and the cottage chimneys, being whipped away by the savage wind. Wind? You don't have mist with wind. It was smoke. It was . . .

'Matt!'

Hal's cry was torn out of him.

'Matt . . . Oh God, let me be in time; let me be in time . . .'

'Bodger, go home. Home! Get help . . .'

Matt was frantic.

But what could the dog do? Who would understand? And he wouldn't be in time. If only he had a rope. Rope. Maybe he could . . . But there was one, hanging on the wall, if he could reach it . . . Rotten, it was bound to be rotten.

'Jump, Matt; go on, love . . . just jump. It'll be all right.'

'But I've got to get *you* out, Granny. I've *got* to. I should have told someone, I should have . . .'

'Matt, stop it.' Granny Apple's voice was firm, though her body shook even in the heat. 'Stop it. Everything is my fault, not yours. Do you understand? Not yours . . . Now, please, child, you must jump. Jump quickly, otherwise . . .'

'No, not yet. I can reach it, if . . . that's got it.'

The old rope tumbled off some high projection, lay in dirty, snaky coils at his feet.

'Love, there isn't time. You go. You mustn't worry about me.'

'Put your arms up – *up*, I said. Oh go on, Granny; don't waste time.' Matt jerked one arm up and began to knot the rope under her armpits, tugging it to make sure it didn't slip. 'Come on; oh, come on . . .'

Tottering together on the bales, peering into the gloom

outside, Granny Apple still begged Matt to jump without her.

'It won't bear two. It can't. Matt dear, there's no time...'

The whole of the centre of the barn was a blazing red furnace, clouds of smoke spreading and rising about them.

'Matt! Matt!' Hal had barely enough breath to whisper, let alone shout. 'Matt! Are you there?'

He stood with the frantic Bodger below the window, balanced precariously on the rubble. Even as he yelled, he looked about him for some means of reaching the window where now Matt's head appeared. His cheeks were fiery with the heat, the skin stretched and taut around his aching eyes, the tattered sacks slipped away.

'Matt, hang on; I'll get you out. Try not to breathe. Can you climb out on to the ledge? ... What? ... What lady? I don't understand.'

'Hal, we've got to her out!'

With a sudden effort, Matt lugged the old lady up in his arms.

Dimly through the smoke that billowed out, Hal could see a tiny face, framed in white hair; she was saying something. He couldn't hear her.

'Keep close to the window. Put your heads out if you can. Matt, you get out, on to the ledge ... Rope? What rope? ... Is it strong enough? ... Is there a beam to run it round? Smooth, it'll have to be smooth or the rope will break. Pad it with something, your anorak will do, or a sack; anything ... and don't panic!'

Don't panic, indeed! Hal was beside himself! He raced round the corner. A ladder, there must be a ladder; something. Anything. A gate – surely he had seen an old gate, wooden. In the nettles. But it wouldn't be tall enough, would it? Even on its end? Better than nothing, and it was close, just there. Careful now. Scrambling about, tugging it free, he dragged it below the window. He could climb up some way, somehow, steady whoever came first. But it might break, or the rope. Soft landing; he must make a soft landing ... But time was nearly gone. Bales, oh for some bales. There were two or three mouldering by an old water-butt; would they break? Could he move them?

He clawed at them in desperation ... hopeless. He found a length of fence under his hand and levered a bale across: it was breaking apart as it went. Just a spread over the jagged tiles and bricks ... two more. And his anorak. No more time.

It was a nightmare.

'Ready?'

Matt nodded, too terrified to speak, his face seeming to sway in the high window.

'OK; come on, then ... What's her name?'

'Granny Apple.'

'Granny ... oh well, it doesn't matter now. Let the rope out slowly; slowly ... push her free. Just let yourself go. I'll reach you soon. Try to go limp.'

The little bundle that hung on the end of the rope, inching down, began to swing, to spin.

'A bit quicker, Matt. Just a touch – that's enough. I've nearly got her, I ... Look out!'

Matt couldn't stop coughing. His eyes felt raw and, although he had backed as near to the window as he could get, the heat was agony. He fixed his mind on the rope, on his hands holding the rope, paying it out, slowly, slowly, over the beam. His gloves were gone; the backs of his hands seemed on fire; his face seemed alight ...

'I can't ... I can't stand it.' Matt began to shake. A

whimper broke from him. 'I can't ...'

Flames leapt up under his feet; but it wasn't the flames that sent him staggering backwards. For a split second he saw the charred and broken rope, a dead thing dangling in his hands, and then he fell. Backwards ...

Hal watched helpless, the old lady crushed in one arm, the other flung out instinctively as the rope snapped. Matt hurtled down towards him, landing with a sickening thud on his back. Then he lay still, his head just off Hal's anorak.

Bodger, strangely silent, came and licked his face; just twice.

CHAPTER FOURTEEN

For a second, Hal seemed paralysed. Then he leapt to his feet, leaving the old lady sagging, limp, against the gate. Her eyes were closed.

'Matt ... Matt, are you ...' He couldn't say it. Bending over the still figure, Hal found the thin wrist, still warm. Pulse; was there a pulse? His own heart was making so much noise, his own hands shook so, he wasn't sure.

'Oh Bodger, stop it ...' Bodger was standing there, head low, whimpering in desolation. 'Bodger, no ...' The dog began to paw at Matt's shoulder, bent to lick again the motionless face ...

Suddenly the body on the ground gave a convulsive shudder, drew a few difficult, rasping lungfuls of air; winded, he was only winded.

A few minutes later, when Matt, though shaky, seemed to have some wits about him, Hal became aware of the scene around him. The window slits of the barn belched grey-black smoke; thin snow was still driving along the wind, stinging their ears. It was cold even under the wall. Out of its shelter, debris whirled and danced, dusk was gathering and it was more than time to move. If they could.

Hal's legs trembled and seemed unwilling to hold him up.

'Are you OK? Can you walk? Maybe you shouldn't try, but . . . is anything broken?'

'I . . . don't think so. I . . . my back hurts, but it's . . . ouch!' Matt bit his lip on a groan. 'It hurts to straighten up, really hurts . . . I don't think I can move; if I try . . .' Matt fell away in a dead faint.

'Matt . . .' No answer.

The old lady. He hadn't even thought of the old lady. Who was she? What on earth had Matt been doing in there?

With a dazed shake of his head, Hal went across. The old lady lolled in a half-sitting-up position, her eyes closed. Her skin was a dirty grey apart from the bright flushes of fever high on the cheek bones. Her breathing was shallow, uneven, her lips dry. Shrunk away inside the charred dressing-gown, there seemed nothing of her. Her hands and feet were bare and blue with cold.

Hal stood in an agony of indecision. He could only help one at a time; he doubted if he could carry either far. They needed shelter, warmth, while he went to fetch help. He had no shelter or warmth to give them. The barn might even collapse; they couldn't stay where they were. But where was he to put them? Matt shouldn't be moved, not with back injuries; that much he knew.

Bodger. If he tied a note to Bodger's collar, would he go home? Would anyone read it? He searched his pockets. No paper, no pencil.

He could move the old lady, wrap her in his coat, perhaps pad it up with straw. That was not too difficult.

But would she stay put? Or would she come to and wander off? Surely not; she seemed too far gone for that, but ... maybe she would wander to the barn and it would fall on her; or maybe to the stream. Or maybe ... He turned his mind away ... Then there was Matt. What, what was he going to do with Matt? He couldn't move him, he couldn't leave him.

Bodger barked. Barked again.

'Shut up, Bodge. I've got to think ...'

Again.

'Bodger! Be quiet!'

But Bodger took no notice. He stood tense, looking along the side of the barn. His tail began to swing, slowly at first, and then more quickly. Voices.

'Hello? Anyone there? Is everything all right?' A man's voice, and then a boy's, an eager shout. 'It's Bodger! Dad, it's Bodger! I'm sure it is; I told you ... Matt! Matt, can you hear me? Come on, Dad, come *on*!'

Footsteps came running, pounding the frozen ground. It was Guppy, Guppy and The Vapouriser. What on earth had brought them here, and brought them now? But there was no time to ask. Guppy hurtled round the angle of the barn, then pulled up short, his eyes wide with horror.

'Matt! Hal, what's happened ... is he ... is he ...' Guppy swallowed.

'No, he winded himself when he fell. He's hurt, but ...'

'Fell? Fell from up there?' Guppy looked up, saw the flames lapping the edges of the brick, and '... up there?' he whispered.

Hal nodded.

'Matt ... Hal, are you sure he isn't ...'

'Dead? No, but he's hurt his back and I don't know how to move him. I shouldn't move him at all, but the wall may ...'

'It won't fall.' Guppy's father stood behind them,

95

solid, and somehow comforting. 'It won't fall, Hal. It's a straw fire – it'll burn out soon.'

'Dad, Matt's ... Matt's just ...'

'Yes. Let's have a look at him.'

As Guppy's father knelt to put a hand on his forehead, Matt's eyes flickered open.

'Where ... where am ... You're ...' His eyes focussed on the dog-collar, gleaming white in the gathering dark. 'You're a vicar! Am I ...' his eyes clouded, 'am I in heaven?'

Hal and Guppy laughed, or maybe they cried. They weren't sure.

'No such luck, Matt, old son. It's only me.'

'Only ...? Oh, I see; it's you. What ... what are you doing ...' His eyes began to close; he opened them with a great effort. 'What are you ... doing here?'

'Oh, this and that.' The Reverend Pilbeam pulled off his coat and tucked it around Matt; he settled Matt's head on Guppy's scarf. 'You just have a quick snooze while we see how to get you home. OK?' But Matt didn't even hear him. He was unconscious again.

'What about her ...'

Hal turned away from his brother, looked at the little bundle against the foot of the wall. She was quite motionless.

'Her?' Guppy's father was puzzled. 'What "her"? What are you talking about?'

'There.' Hal pointed, started towards her.

'Who is she?' Mr Pilbeam unconsciously lowered his voice, as if he feared to wake her. He clambered over the rubble and bent over the still, cold shape.

'Hal, who is she? What's been happening?'

'I don't know. I don't know anything. Matt was ... in there.' He shuddered, his face white, his eyes too large for his face. Suddenly he had to sit down. 'She ... she

96

was in there, with Matt. He was trying to get her out, and . . . he fell. On his back . . . But she's wearing a dressing-gown. Why is she wearing a dressing-gown? I don't . . . it doesn't make sense.'

There seemed no breath of life now in the little old lady.

Mr Pilbeam was very quiet. Crouching beside the still form, his fingers felt for her pulse. He put his face close to hers, trying to detect some trace of breath. Nothing. Nothing at all.

'Did she fall?'

'No; well, only a little way . . . sort of on to me. But she hasn't . . . hasn't moved since.'

Mr Pilbeam looked grave and old; old, thought Hal, vaguely surprised.

Guppy hadn't said another word. He sat a little way off, a tiny statue, one hand on Bodger's neck, his eyes fixed on Matt's unconscious face.

'Well . . .,' Guppy's father straightened, braced himself for action, 'either we leave them here while somebody goes for help, or we carry this one – she surely can't weigh much, she's just a bag of bones – or . . .' He paused, thinking, tapping his teeth with a fingernail. 'It's so cold; cold enough to . . . OK. Matt stays; I'm not moving him with that back. Hal, you must stay with him . . . Yes, I know; don't worry – the flames are not so fierce, they're burning out. Nothing's going to fall on you. Just keep calm and keep Matt still if he comes to; whatever you do, don't let him try to sit up, or even to move. Where's your coat? You're shivering. Gareth, give your anorak to Hal . . . quickly now . . .'

The boys looked at him. Give the anorak to . . .?

'Oh. Yes, I . . .' Guppy began to struggle out of it, 'I see.'

'But I can't . . . you . . .' Hal was still incapable of clear thinking.

97

'Go on, biff. Shove it on.' Guppy thrust his coat at him. 'Not like that, you 'nana; here, put your arm in here . . .'

'But . . .'

'That's it; help him, Gareth.'

With an effort, Hal put on Guppy's coat, still shaking with cold or shock, both maybe. The Vapouriser was right; Guppy could run on ahead, fetch help; coat or no coat, the cold wouldn't kill him. As for himself, he was needed here. Matt needed him.

Guppy's father bent again, caught up . . . who was it? Granny Apple, was it, Matt had called her? . . . carried her slowly, carefully, trying to hold some warmth around the tiny form. He had on more layers than Guppy even now, even without his thick coat which lay, lightly powdered with snow, over Matt.

'What about Bodger?' The dog was shivering, quiet apart from an occasional thin whimper. 'Will you take him?' That was Hal.

Mr Pilbeam looked at the older boy's white face, his eyes . . .

'No,' he said gently. 'No. Bodger will stay with you. With both of you. He wouldn't come anyway.' He smiled a little. 'Give him a hug, Hal; he's a very worried fellow, he doesn't understand.'

Hal moved across to the dog, finding surprising comfort in his big body, his single-minded loyalty.

'It's OK, Bodge, it's OK.' He could feel Bodger trembling under his hand. He put an arm around the broad shoulders, played with the fur on the dog's chest. 'It's OK, Bodge; he's just . . . asleep.' Hal caught his breath, pulled the dog closer, 'He's just asleep.'

They settled down to their vigil, the two of them; almost unaware of the little party setting off up the track. Guppy raced away into the dark. His father moved slowly after him, Granny Apple's body held against his shoulder, her hair just catching the fading light of the flames.

'Hal . . .' He paused; the old lady's hand swung like an old rag. 'Hal . . .' but his eyes were on Matt, lying in the snow. Why didn't he stir, open his eyes? 'Hal, you must keep him warm, as warm as you can.'

Then, so low that the words ebbed away into the night, 'Matt, old son, don't . . .'

He didn't finish.

CHAPTER FIFTEEN

Hal lost all sense of time. His mind seemed suspended in a no-man's land, swinging backwards and forwards, catching at wisps and snatches of memory. Pictures flickered behind his eyes: Matt straightening too anxiously from his bed, Matt's closed face after the night excursion, his sudden anxieties. How long had he known Granny Apple and where had he found her? What had he been doing?

Incongruous thoughts surfaced, odd thoughts. 'I should be doing my biology; genes, I'm sure it was something to do with genes.' He tried to remember, worried that he couldn't, and then as suddenly abandoned it.

He put out his hand to touch Matt's face, cold, clammy. Bodger stirred, looked up at him, instantly catching his fear.

'Keep him warm; how can I keep him warm?' Hal looked about him; was there anything? If he could only keep the wind off a little. He moved round to sit on the windward side, leaning over as protection.

'Bodger, lie down. Lie!'

Bodger didn't want to lie down.

'Come on, Bodge; here ... you could keep him warm. Lie!'

Reluctantly Bodger allowed himself to be persuaded, uneasy at this strange, still game. Hal stroked him, over and over, soothing, calming. 'Good dog, good Bodge ... no, keep still. Good boy ...'

How long would they be? Hal tried to work it out. It would take Guppy ten minutes perhaps, maybe a quarter of an hour, if he ran non-stop. Then five minutes to make someone understand, to grab a phone, to call for help. How long would an ambulance take – would it be an ambulance? A doctor, maybe. But how would they reach the barn, stuck out here in the fields, isolated, beyond the stream. The track was hopeless, overgrown and broken, far too bumpy for Matt ... Oh come *on*, come *on* ...

Hours seemed to pass.

'Matt ... Matt, can you hear me?'

Somewhere Hal had read that hearing was the last of the senses to go.

'Matt. You'll be OK; you'll ...' What was that? A flicker, a beam of light, first up in the sky, then down, then hidden by a fold of the ground. It disappeared altogether, came back, not on the village side of the barn at all.

He could hear something, some sort of motor, an engine – 'Matt, wake up; wake up! They're coming. Here! Here! We're over here!' He stood up and shouted, waving his arms wildly above his head; then he sat down, suddenly thinking what a fool he was. Nobody could see him in the dark! 'Idiot,' he told himself sternly. 'Idiot!' But at the same time he felt a lightness and a warmth steal through his cramped body; the beginnings of a smile crept about his eyes.

Bodger added his bit to the rescue bid. 'Woof! Woof! The noise crashed in waves against the wall of the barn, rang out over the wind. The cloaking dark was all at once a sheltering hand.

All they had to do was to wait.

Minutes later, a mud-spattered Land Rover nosed into the old yard, crunching across the broken tiles which snapped like gunshot, blinding Hal with its lurching headlights.

'Where is he?' Dimly, Hal was aware that someone was tumbling out of the passenger seat, stumbling across. Dr Blair. Behind him Mr Agnew, the farmer, climbed down, holding a case.

'Is he . . . is he all right?'

'Let's have a wee look. Keep those headlights on, Jim . . . Good man. Here, pass it over . . . Now, laddie, let's just see . . .'

Quietly, methodically, Dr Blair began to run experimental hands over Matt's body, feeling, checking. He took out a torch, opened an eyelid, flicked the switch. Matt flinched, murmured.

'He's alive, he's alive!' Hal shouted it.

Dr Blair permitted himself a slow smile. 'Aye, he's alive right enough. You'll no be rid of the wee rascal that easily, I'm thinking. I'll no shift him; he'll bide fine where he is till the ambulance comes by. I'll just give him a wee shot, just a wee shot . . .'

Matt didn't remember much about the ambulance, the journey; his head didn't seem to work too well. He remembered lights and men's voices, strong hands lifting him, waves of pain, a red blanket. They wheeled him in and out of pools of brightness, of shadows, down long corridors, through shining doors; they slid him under strange grey machines, turned him, marooned him in space; the voices all seemed far away, all gentle, reassuring . . .

His parents sat with him a little while; cups of tea appeared from nowhere, he took some pills.

Sleepy and warm, it all came tumbling out, all of it. There were unexpected tears in his mother's eyes as she hung over him.

'If Hal hadn't come . . . or Guppy . . .' His eyes grew suddenly dark with fear, with . . .

'Don't think of it, Matt. It's behind you; over. Just think about getting well.'

'Am I . . . will I . . .' Matt hesitated, stumbled over the words, 'will I . . . walk again?'

His father took hold of his hand, comforting, calm.

'Don't worry; it's too soon. You're in the best possible place. It won't be long before we know . . . And whatever happens, whatever happens, Matt, you're with us; we're still here. You're not alone. Together . . .'

'We're so proud of you, so . . .' His mother's voice was not quite steady.

There was a little silence. Matt choked back a sob; what if he never walked again? What if . . . Better not to think of it. Better to think of something else, of Granny Apple.

'Is she . . . alive?'

'Yes, my love, she's alive. She's in another ward here, sleeping. She's absolutely exhausted, in deep shock. It will take a day or two to know how ill she is, if she will ever . . .'

Matt remembered her leg, that dreadful wound.

'It was horrible, it was all yukky.'

'What was?'

'Her leg; it . . .' He felt sick.

'Oh, Matt, don't. Don't worry. You did all you could. She'd probably have died by now if you hadn't found her, kept her warm, fed her; you cleaned that . . . You gave her something more . . .'

'More?' Matt was puzzled. The lights seemed to be behaving oddly, first coming nearer, brighter, then fading away, fading . . .

'Try to sleep.'

His eyelids were heavy, too heavy to lift. Someone murmured something. He didn't hear.

Time passed.

Back home it was almost midnight. Hal looked dead on his feet; Bridgie yawned, tired out, propping her head on both hands.

'I wish they'd ring; it's awful, not knowing. Hal, do you think . . . No, it doesn't matter.' Bridgie fell silent.

'Do I think what?'

'Do you think it's all right or aren't they ringing because . . . well, because Matt's . . .'

'I don't know.'

They looked at each other, then looked away. After a while, 'Hal, are they coming back tonight? Maybe we should go to bed, but . . .,' Bridgie's voice faltered, 'I can't . . . not yet. It . . . it seems awful just to go to bed as if nothing's happened.'

'They'll come back; one of them, anyway. It's just . . . I don't know how long X-rays take; maybe Matt needs some treatment, some operation. They'd stay for that. Unless . . . Bodger, what *is* it? Stop pushing like that, you'll have me over.'

Bodger whined. He went and pawed at the door.

'What do you want, Bodge?'

The dog turned an accusing, sorrowful face upon them, gave a short bark.

'What . . . oh, Bodge! Bodge, you poor fellow; we forgot you. Come on, then. Bridgie, he hasn't had his food . . .'

Why didn't they ring?

Just for a moment Matt woke.

The hospital bed was strangely tight, the sheets binding him down were too crisp, too white. Lying there, Matt caught a brief glimpse of his father as he disappeared round a screen at the end of the ward. Then he was gone. The lights were dim, the people in the other beds seemed to be asleep, though someone was coughing, a thin, weak sound.

He felt sleepy and his eyes kept slipping out of focus . . .

CHAPTER SIXTEEN

Matt seemed different, somehow. 'More grown-up ... is that it?' Hal wondered. 'More settled?'

'He's changed.' Everyone could see that, but 'We've changed, too.' That was Bridgie.

'*We've* changed? How come, how've we changed ... I don't get it.'

'Well, we have ... We ...' Bridgie found it difficult to explain. 'We sort of ... oh, I don't know ... respect him. Well, not respect exactly, but ... well, he's just surprising ...' And that was as close as they ever got to putting it into words.

Matt had a new confidence, a new calm, a new ... 'He's happy,' said Hal.

He was. Matt could not remember ever feeling so at peace with the world, with himself. Walking down the street, a bunch of flowers in one hand and a carefully wrapped parcel in the other, there was a lilt in his walk; except when he remembered Granny Apple. Would she know him? Would she need him any more? Little Granny Apple. All these weeks. The bandages had gone from his hands, the burn marks fading. The stiffness in his back was a thing of the past; the bruises, though spectacular, were painless. His friends pestered him for details, but he was oddly reluctant to play the hero. Guppy was frankly envious but ... Matt gave an involuntary shiver ... he could not go through that again, not ever.

All the mysteries had fallen away; just an old lady, shocked, bewildered. What chance had brought her to Gallows End? If it were chance. The Vapouriser thought not; he said she was 'taken by the hand', and refused to go into details. Then his eyes had twinkled and he had said something about 'a lost sheep'.

'Sheep? Granny Apple? Not a sheep ...' Matt remembered quite clearly. 'It was a bear.'

The Vapouriser merely grinned, ruffled Matt's hair. 'You'll do. I'll get you in the end ...'

'Get me?'

'Get you. I'm nearer than you think!'

Potty, that's what he was. Potty. Guppy's father was going round the twist. Ah, well; bad luck on Guppy!

But what was this bear business? He had sorted out everything else. Thinking back, he did have a vague memory of something on the news, that first weekend. Somebody lost; a fire. It was Granny Apple. She had been visiting her grandchildren, Charlie and ... Sarah, was it? Yes, Sarah. There had been this fire, a terrible fire. Granny Apple had gone back in, back in to Charlie's room. She was so brave, his old lady. They had tried to stop her; Charlie was safely out anyway, but she had pulled free, plunged into the smoke, choking, determined. They had got her out of course, somehow, but then ... she had gone. Disappeared. Vanished; and in her dressing-gown. Police, news flashes; no sign.

It was obvious now. The sticky brown holes, they were burns. The tatty slippers; well, she had wandered miles in them, cross-country, all the time confused, searching. Her fear of fire was explained – why hadn't he noticed it? It was clear enough ... the mind-blowing shock, the blisters, weeping, everything. So obvious.

'But why didn't you tell us? Didn't you think it strange? We could have helped, found out who she was.'

Did his parents not see?

'I couldn't. You wouldn't have believed me.'

'Oh Matt . . .'

'I couldn't give her away. I didn't know . . . and . . .?' – this was the wonderful thing – 'it was me she wanted . . .' Wanted. How often had people wanted Matt? Again and again Matt had gone over those few days, his family fascinated, absorbed. His mother had kept hugging him, dropping kisses on his head in passing. 'Oh, Mum, gerroff!' All that planning, the cold, the fears, the risks, that . . . could you call it love? Matt shied away from the word, embarrassed, but . . . what else could you call it? That closeness, that protecting, that ache . . .

'I stole some money.' He had had to tell them. It was strange; they almost seemed not to mind, although he knew, as they knew, that it was wrong. 'It's *why* you do something that matters, Matt, much more than what you do.' That's what they had said. Maybe. Anyway, he was paying it back out of his pocket-money.

But he still had not found out about the bear.

Gosh, was he here already? He felt a little nervous. Where did he have to go in? Outpatients? No, that didn't seem right. Visitors; that's it. Visitors.

The hospital seemed huge, noisy. There were people everywhere. It echoed. He wished that Hal and Bridgie were with him. Or Bodge.

Five minutes later he looked carefully into Ward 3. 'Hastings' it said on the door. Hastings? That was a battle; at least . . . 'Oh, it doesn't matter,' Matt muttered to himself. He was dreadfully embarrassed, red to the tips of his ears and crushing the flowers.

'Hi, son. Looking for someone?' She wore a dark blue dress, a white apron; she paused beside him for a moment. 'Are you lost?'

'No, I don't think so. This is Ward 3, isn't it?'

'That's right. Who are you looking for?'

'Granny Apple.' It was out before he realized. He blushed again; he hadn't a clue what her real name was.

'Your granny, love? Just walk in; you'll find her.' She smiled, walked away.

'Will I?' thought Matt. 'Will I find her?' His hands were sticky, hot. He started cautiously forward, looking at everyone but trying not to stare too hard.

It was a women's ward. Some were obviously very ill, lying still and white on the pillows, laced with tubes and charts. Some sat quietly, not looking at anything, waiting. For visitors? There were lots of visitors about, brisk, cheerful, surrounded by bags. One bent over a locker, arranging flowers, smiling encouragement. She looks nice, thought Matt, pretty for an old lady; not even very old, despite the white hair arranged in a smooth pleat at the back of her head. 'Pretty neat,' decided Matt. Slim and elegant in a heather-coloured outfit, little heels to her shoes, a silver bracelet. 'Pretty neat.' Matt almost spoke aloud. Still, he had not come here to admire trendy visitors of uncertain age. Granny Apple. Where was Granny Apple?

'I can't even ask,' groaned Matt, inwardly. 'I don't know her name.'

He walked the full length of the ward. He walked back. She wasn't there. Had she gone out? Matt grinned, privately. Not a bush this time! He giggled. The heather lady swung round at the sound, smiled.

'Excuse me, do you know if . . .' Matt stopped. This was going to be difficult. He swallowed, fixed his eyes on the little heeled shoes. 'That is, I'm looking for someone; a lady. A little old lady. But I don't know her name, and . . .'

'I do.'

Startled, Matt looked up at the heather lady. In her eyes lurked a mischievous twinkle, a familiar . . .

'Granny! Granny Apple! It's you . . . it can't be you. You look . . . I mean . . . but you're not old.'

'Thank you. That's quite the nicest thing anyone's said to me today. Mr Stephenson said you were a charmer . . .'

'Mr Stephenson? Who's Mr Stephenson?'

'He teaches you, or so he tells me.'

'Mr Stephenson? Old Fungus? I mean . . .' Matt broke off in confusion.

Granny Apple grinned appreciatively.

'Ah, the beard, I suppose.'

'How do you know . . . what does old . . . Mr Stephenson have to do with you?'

'I talked to him. On the telephone. He came to see me yesterday, on his way home.'

'But why? I mean he's OK, but . . .'

'I hear you're reading *A Town Like Alice*.'

'Yes, but . . .'

'Do you like it?'

'Yes; well, it's OK, I suppose. The jungle bit was pretty scary.'

'Australia can be pretty scary, too; but it's beautiful, Matt. You'd love it.'

They were back at her bed by now. She sat down, stood Matt straight before her, holding him lightly by the shoulders. The trembling, the head-bobbing, all had gone.

'Mr Stephenson thinks you'd love it. Your vicar, too.'

'My vicar? Do you know *every*body I know?'

'Well, I haven't met Gareth – sorry, Guppy – yet, but give me time.'

It was all beyond Matt. He remembered his presents.

'Those are for you.' He thrust out the flowers, the little

parcel.

'They're lovely, Matt. Thank you.' She bent down to smell the faint, clean scent of the narcissi. She laid them gently down and began to untie the little oblong packet.

'I didn't know what you'd like, so ... Anyway, I couldn't think of anything else.' Matt looked anxious.

The ribbons fell away.

'Oh Matt, that's perfect. Do you know, I can't find any here.'

The shiny pack of new playing-cards glistened under the ward lights.

'Open that drawer, Matt, will you?'

He did as she asked.

'Now, take out that envelope. Go on; open it.'

Matt carefully pulled out the flap, slid out a fat travel catalogue. It was of Australia.

'That's for you.'

'For me? Why for me? What's it for?'

'It's a thank-you and a promise.'

'How ... a promise?'

'Sit down, just here. Now listen carefully because I'm only going to say this once. In Australia I have a son, and this summer I'm going out to see him, for six weeks. And I would like you, Matt, to come too. Will you? I'm really quite a capable granny in my own quiet way, barring accidents, and ... well, I'd like you to come. Jack's son is just your age; he's called Simon. Well?'

'Granny Apple, I ... it's ... oh, Granny Apple! It's an ace idea, it's ...' he fished out some vague memory, some film echo, 'it's good on yer!'

Granny Apple collapsed, helpless with laughter.

'Oh Matt, that's ...' she wiped her eyes, 'that's ... fair dinkum!' They shrieked with mirth, clutching each other, oblivious of everyone.

'Hmm.' The staff nurse looked on. 'It's time she went home.'

*

Later, over their fifth game of gin rummy, Matt remembered.

'Granny Apple, why did you keep on about a bear? All the time . . .'

'Did I? Well,' Granny Apple frowned a little, trying to get it clear in her mind, 'that's what I went back to fetch. Last time I was in Australia, Charlie was only a baby. I brought him back a toy koala bear. He adored it, still does. It's practically bald now, he's hugged it so much. He never goes to bed without it, never; so I . . . well, I just had to rescue it.'

'And did you?'

'I don't remember; I just don't remember. We'll get another, we'll get two or three, a whole sackful. And there's another thing; I am not Granny Apple, you know. I do have a name.' She smiled – quite wickedly, it seemed to Matt.

'What is it? Hi, Mum.'

The whole family had arrived to fetch him home, smiling, proud.

'Get this . . .' She paused, dramatically. 'It's Mrs Berrington de Sales la Fontaine, without hyphens.'

'It's . . . Granny Apple, you're an idiot.'

'But it's true!'

'Tough. You're Granny Apple.'